Wythe Grayson R... W9-AYW-559
Independence, Virginia

THE
DARK
SHORE

THE
DARK
SHORE

SUSAN HOWATCH

𝔰𝔡

STEIN AND DAY/*Publishers*/New York

To my mother,
who first took me to Cornwall,
and to Brenda and Sally,
who first came with me to Clougy.

Copyright © 1965 by Susan Howatch
Library of Congress Catalog Card No. 70-185884
All rights reserved
Published simultaneously in Canada by Saunders of Toronto Ltd.
Printed in the United States of America
Stein and Day/*Publishers*/7 East 48 Street, New York, N.Y. 10017
ISBN 0-8128-1457-6
Any resemblance of the characters herein described to persons
living or dead is purely coincidental.

THIRD PRINTING, 1972

Prologue

JON WAS ALONE. Outside in the night the city teemed and throbbed and roared but in the room there was only the quiet impersonal silence of the hotel room, softly-lit and thick-carpeted. He went over to the window. Six floors below him to the left a bus crawled north up Berkeley Street, a noiseless fleck of red against the dark surface of the road, while immediately below him the swarms of taxis cruised past the hotel entrance before turning south towards Piccadilly. The sense of isolation was accentuated by the stillness in the room. The polish on the furniture gleamed; the white pillowcases on the bed were spotlessly smooth; the suitcases stood martialed along the wall in faultless formation. He was alone in a vast city, a stranger returning to a forgotten land, and it seemed to him as he stood by the window and stared out at the world beyond that he had been foolish to hope that he could establish any contact with the past by coming back to the city where he had been born.

He spent ten minutes unpacking the basic items from his luggage and then paused to light a cigarette. Below him on the bed lay the evening paper, his own photograph still smiling up at him from the gossip column, and as he picked up the paper again in contempt he was conscious of a stab of unreality, as if the photograph was of someone else and the lines beneath described a man he did not know. They called him a Canadian, of course, and

7

said he was a millionaire. There was a line mentioning his mother too and her connection with pre-war London society, a final sentence adding that he was to remarry shortly and that his fiancée was English. And then the columnist passed on to other topics, confident that he had fully exploited the snob value of this particular visitor to London.

Jon tore the newspaper to shreds and thought of his mother. She would have read it an hour, perhaps two hours ago, when the evening paper was delivered to the spacious house off Halkin Street. So she would know. He wondered if she had any desire to see him, any shred of interest in meeting him again after ten years. He had never written to her. When he had told Sarah that he and his mother no longer kept in touch with each other she had been so shocked that he had felt embarrassed, but justification had been easy and he had thought no more about it. Sarah simply did not understand. She had grown up in a happy sheltered home, and any deviation from the pattern of life which she had always known only emphasized how vulnerable she was when separated from that narrow comfortable little backwater her parents had created for her. One of the reasons why he wanted to marry Sarah was because she was untouched and unspoiled by the world he lived and worked in every day. When they were married, he thought, he would work all day in an atmosphere of boardrooms and balance sheets, and then at last he would be home away from it all and Sarah would be waiting for him. . . . He could see it all so clearly. Sarah would talk of the things he loved and after dinner he would play the piano, and there would be a still cool peace as night fell. And afterwards when they were in bed he would let her know how grateful he was to her for that wonderful peace, and Sarah would love him because he was her shield from the harshest flares of life and she needed him even more than he needed her.

It would all be so different from the past.

He thought of Sophia then, the memory flashing through his brain in the split second before he shut his mind against it. He mustn't think of Sophia. He would not, could not think of her. . . . But he was. While he was in London he would meet Justin and as soon as he saw Justin he would think of Sophia. . . . Nonsense. Justin was a young Englishman nineteen years old with the conventional English background of public school and perhaps a first job in the city. He would think of sports cars and parties and pretty girls and cricket in summer. Justin would be as utterly remote from Sophia as London was from Toronto, and on meeting him again there would be no cruel memories of the past, no dreadful searing pain.

The telephone rang.

The jangling bell was obscene, blasting aside the still silence of the room and making Jon start. Slumping onto the bed he reached for the receiver and leaned back against the pillows.

"Yes?"

"Call for you, Mr. Towers."

"Thank you."

There was a click, and then a silence except for the humming of the wire.

"Hullo?" He was tense suddenly, taut with nervousness.

Another pause. Someone far away at the other end of the wire took a small shallow breath.

"Hullo?" Jon said again. "Who's this?" There was ice suddenly, ice on his forehead, at the nape of his neck, at the base of his spine, although he didn't know why he was afraid.

9

And then very softly the anonymous voice from the past whispered into the receiver, "Welcome home, Mr. Towers. Does your fiancée know how you killed your first wife ten years ago?"

I

One

I

Justin Towers very nearly didn't buy an evening paper. When he left the office at half-past five his eyes were tired after hours spent poring over figures and the prospect of his return journey on the underground filled him with a violent revulsion. He hated the rush hour tubes, hated being crammed into the long sweating corridors, hated the endless stream of faceless people who jostled past him in the subterranean nightmare. He thought for a long aching moment of his childhood, of the days beneath blue skies by a swaying sea, of the yellow walls and white shutters of Clougy, and then the moment was past and he was standing irresolutely by one of the innumerable entrances to the underground at Bank while the diesel fumes choked his lungs and the traffic roared in his ears. Across the road a number nine bus crawled on its way to Ludgate Circus. Justin made up his mind quickly; as the traffic lights changed he crossed Poultry and Queen Victoria Street and boarded the bus as it wedged itself deep in a line of stationary cars.

By the time the bus reached Green Park he was so sick of the constant waiting and the frustration of the traffic jams that he got out and walked towards the tube without hesitation. He felt desparetely tired, and in an attempt to stave off the tedium of the last stretch of the journey he stopped by the newsvendor's stall and bought an evening paper.

He opened it on the platform, glanced at the stock exchange prices and then folded it up again as a train drew in. On finding a small corner at one end of the compartment he glanced at the front page, but he was conscious of his hatred of the crowded train once more and he thinking not of the paper in his hand but of Clougy on those bright summer afternoons long ago. The scene etched itself clearly in his mind. Flip would be lying on his back, his long tail waving gracefully and the lawn would be soft and green and smooth. From the open windows of the house would come the sound of a piano being touched softly on light keys, and on the wrought-iron white swing-seat across the lawn a woman would be lying relaxed with a bowl of cherries on the wrought-iron table nearby. If he were to venture towards her and ask for a cherry the woman would yawn a wide, rich yawn and smile a warm, luxurious smile and say indulgently in her strange English, "But you'll get so fat, Justin!" And then she would pull him closer to her so that she could kiss him and afterwards she would let him have as many cherries as he wanted.

The hunger of those days was one of the things he remembered best. He had always been hungry, and the days had been full of Cornish cream and Cornish pasties until one evening the man, who would spend so many hours of a beautiful day indoors with a piano, said to him that it was time they both had some exercise before Justin became too fat to move. After that they had fallen into the habit of walking down to the cove together after tea. Further along the cliff path that curled away from the cove were the Flat Rocks by the water's edge, and they would go down there together, the man helping the child over the steeper parts of the cliff. It was a stiff climb. The shore was scored with vast boulders and gi-

14

gantic slabs of granite, and after the scramble to the water's edge they would lie in the sun for a while and watch the endless motion of the sea as it sucked and spat at the rocky shelves beneath them. Sometimes the man would talk. Justin loved it when he talked. The man would paint pictures in words for him, and suddenly the world would be rich and exciting and full of bright colors. Sometimes the man wouldn't talk at all, which was disappointing, but the excitement was still there because the man was exciting in himself and whenever Justin was with him it seemed that even a walk to the cove and the Flat Rocks could be transformed into a taut racing adventure pounding with life and danger and anticipation. The man seemed to enjoy the walks too. Even when they had people staying at Clougy there would come times when he would want to get away from them all and then Justin had been his only companion, the chosen confidant to share the hours of seclusion.

Justin, immensely proud of his position, would have followed him to the ends of the earth.

And then had come that other weekend, creeping stealthily out of a cloudless future and suddenly the world was gray and streaked with pain and bewilderment and grief. . . .

Afterwards, all he could remember was his grandmother, looking very smart and elegant in a light blue suit. "You're going to come and live with me now, darling —won't that be nice? So much nicer for you to live in London instead of some dreary little place at the back of beyond . . . What? But didn't your father explain it to you? No, of course you can't go abroad with him! He wants you to grow up in England and have a proper education, and anyway he doesn't want a nine-year-old child with him wherever he goes. Surely you can see that. . . .

Why hasn't he written? Well, darling, because he simply never writes a letter—gracious me, I should know that better than anyone! But he'll send you something at Christmas and on your birthday, I expect. Unless he forgets. That's more than likely, of course. He was always forgetting my birthday when he was away at school. . . ."

And he had forgotten. That was the terrible thing. He had forgotten and Justin had never heard from him again.

The train thundered along the dark tunnel and suddenly he was in the present again with his collar damp against the back of his neck and the newspaper crumpling in his hot hands. Useless to think back. The past was over, closed, forgotten, and he had long ago schooled himself not to waste time feeling bitter. He would never see his father again and now he had no wish to. Any attachment that had ever existed between them had been severed long ago.

The train careered into Hyde Park Station, and as several passengers moved out on to the platform, Justin folded the paper down the center and started to turn each half-page mechanically. The photograph caught his eye less than five seconds later.

"John Towers, the Canadian property millionaire . . ."

The shock was like a white light exploding behind his eyes.

When he got out of the train at Knightsbridge he felt sick and ill as if he had just vomited and he had to sit down for a moment at one of the benches on the platform before fighting his way to the surface. Someone stopped to ask him if he was all right. Outside in the open air he paused for a moment among the swirling crowds on the pavement and then very slowly he threw the evening paper in a litter-bin and started the walk home to his grandmother's house in Consett Mews.

II

In the house in Consett Mews, Camilla opened the top drawer of her dressing-table, took out a small bottle and tipped two white pills into the palm of her hand. It was wrong to take two, of course, but it wouldn't matter once in a while. Doctors were always over-cautious. After she had taken the tablets she returned to the dressing-table and re-applied her make-up carefully, taking especial care with the eyes and with the lines about the mouth, but it seemed to her as she stared into the mirror that the shock still showed in her expression in spite of all the pains she had taken with the cosmetics.

She started to think of Jon again.

If only it were possible to keep it from Justin. . . . Jon was obviously only in England on account of his English fiancée or possibly because of some business reason, and did not intend to see any of his family. It would only hurt Justin to know that his father was in London and would be making no attempts to contact him.

The anger was suddenly a constriction in her throat, an ache behind her eyes. It was monstrous of Jon, she thought, to disown his family casually to the extent of returning to England after ten years without even letting his own mother know he was in the country. "It's not that I want to see him," she said aloud, "I don't give a damn whether he comes to see me or not while he's in London. It's merely the principle of the thing."

The tears were scorching her cheeks again, scarring the

new make-up irrevocably, and in an involuntary movement she stood up and moved blindly over to the window.

Supposing Justin heard his father was in London. Supposing he went to see Jon and was drawn inevitably towards him until he was completely under his father's influence. . . . It was all very well to say that Justin was grown up, a levelheaded sensible young man of nineteen who would hardly be easily influenced by anyone, let alone by a father who had treated him so disgracefully, but Jon was so accustomed to influencing everyone within his reach. . . . If he should want to take Justin away from her—but he wouldn't, of course. What had Jon ever done for Justin? It was she who had brought Justin up. Jon couldn't have cared less. Justin belonged to her, not to Jon, and Jon would realize that as clearly as she did.

She thought of Jon again for one long moment, the memory a hot pain behind her eyes.

He was always the same, she thought. Always. Right from the beginning. All those nursemaids—and none of them could do anything with him. He would never listen to me. He was always struggling to impose his will on everyone else's and do exactly as he liked when he liked how he liked.

She thought of the time when she had sent him to boarding school a year early because she had felt unable to cope with him any longer. He hadn't missed her, she remembered sardonically, but had revelled instead in his independence; there had been new fields to conquer, other boys of his own age to sway or bully, masters to impress or mock as the mood suited him. And then had come the piano.

"My God!" she said aloud to the silent room. "That dreadful piano!" He had seen one when he was five years old, tried to play it and failed. That had been enough. He had never rested after that until he had mastered the instrument completely, and even now she could remember his ceaseless practice and the noise which had constantly set her nerves on edge. And then after the piano, later on in his life, there had been the girls. Every girl had been a challenge; a whole new world of conquest had suddenly materialized before his eyes as he had grown old enough to see it around him. She remembered worrying in case he entangled himself in some impossible scrape, remembered threatening that he would have to go to his father for help if he got into trouble, remembered how much it had hurt when he had laughed, mocking her anger. She could still hear his laugh even now. He hadn't cared! And then when he had only been nineteen there had come the episode with the little Greek bitch in a backstreet restaurant in Soho, the fool-hardy marriage, the casual abandonment of all his prospects in the City. . . . Looking back, she wondered bitterly who had been the angrier, her first husband or herself. Not that Jon had cared how angry they had been. He had merely laughed and turned his back as if his parents had meant even less to him than the future he had so casually discarded, and after that she had hardly ever seen him.

The memories flickered restlessly through her brain: her refusal to accept his wife, Jon's retaliation by moving to the other end of England; after his marriage he had only contacted his mother when it suited him.

When Sophia was dead, for example. He had contacted her then soon enough. "I'm going abroad," he had said. "You'll look after Justin, won't you?"

Just like that. You'll look after Justin, won't you? As if she were some domestic servant being given a casual order.

She had often asked herself why she had said yes. She hadn't intended to. She had wanted to say "Find someone else to do your dirty work for you!" but had instead merely agreed to do as he wished, and then all at once Justin was with her and Jon was in Canada. . . . And he had never once written to her.

She hadn't believed it would be possible for Jon to ignore her so completely. She had not expected to hear from him regularly, but since she had taken charge of his son for him she had expected him to keep him in touch with her. And he had never written her a single letter. She had refused to believe it at first. She had thought, There'll be a letter by the next post; he must surely write this week. But he had never written.

The tears were scalding her cheeks, and she turned swiftly back to the dressing-table again in irritation to repair the make-up.

"It's because I'm so angry," she said to herself as if it were necessary to vindicate herself from any accusation of weakness. "It's because it makes me so angry." It wasn't because she was upset or hurt or anything foolish. It merely made her so angry to think that after all she had done to help him he had never even bothered to write to thank her.

She glanced at her watch. Justin would be home soon. With unsteady, impatient movements she obliterated the tears with a paper tissue and reached for the jar of powder. Speed was very important now. Justin must never see her like this. . . .

As she concentrated once more upon the task of make-up she found herself wondering if anyone had ever heard from Jon once he had gone to Canada. Perhaps he had written to Marijohn. She had heard nothing more of Marijohn since the divorce with Michael. She had not even seen Michael himself since the previous Christmas when they had met unexpectedly at one of the drearier cocktail parties someone had given at that time. . . . She had always been so fond of Michael. Jon had never cared for him, of course, always preferring that dreadful man—what had his name been? She frowned, annoyed at the failure of memory. She could remember so well seeing his name mentioned in the gossip columns of the lower type of daily paper. . . . Alexander, she thought suddenly. That was it. Max Alexander.

From somewhere far away, the latch on the front door clicked and someone stepped into the hall.

He was back.

She put the finishing touches to her make-up, stood up and went out on to the landing.

"Justin?"

"Hullo," he called from the livingroom. He sounded calm and untroubled. "Where are you?"

"Just coming." He doesn't know, she thought. He hasn't seen the paper. It's going to be all right.

She reached the hall and moved into the livingroom. There was a cool draught of air, and over by the long windows the curtains swayed softly in the mellow light.

"Ah, there you are," said Justin.

"How are you, darling? Nice day?"

"Hm-hm."

She gave him a kiss and stood looking at him for a moment. "You don't sound too certain!"

He glanced away, moving over to the fireplace, and picked up a package of cigarettes for a moment before putting them down again and moving towards the long windows.

"Your plants are doing well, aren't they?" he said absently, looking out into the patio, and then suddenly he was swinging round, catching her unawares when she was off her guard, and the tension was in every line of her face and body.

"Justin—?"

"Yes," he said placidly. "I've seen the paper." He strolled over to the sofa, sat down and picked up the *Times*. "The photograph didn't look much like him, did it? I wonder why he's in London." When no reply was forthcoming, he started to glance down the personal column but soon abandoned it for the center pages. The room was filled with the rustle of the newspaper being turned inside out, and then he added, "What's for dinner, G.? Is it steak tonight?"

"Justin darling—" Camilla was moving swiftly over to the sofa, her hands agitated, her voice strained and high. "I know just how you must be feeling—"

"I don't see how you can, G., because to be perfectly honest, I don't feel anything. It means nothing to me at all."

She stared at him. He stared back tranquilly and then glanced back at the *Times*.

"I see," said Camilla, turning away abruptly. "Of course you won't be contacting him."

"Of course not. Will you?" He carefully turned the paper back again and stood up. "I'll be going out after dinner, G.," he said presently, going over to the door. "Back about eleven, I expect. I'll try not to make too much noise when I come in."

"I see," she said slowly. "Yes. Yes, that's all right, Justin."

The door closed gently and she was alone in the silent room. She felt relieved that he seemed to have taken such a sensible view of the situation, but she could not rid herself of her anxiety, and amidst all her confused worries she found herself comparing her grandson's total self-sufficiency with Jon's constant assertion of his independence. . . .

III

Eve never bought an evening paper because there was usually never any time to read it. The journey from her office in Piccadilly to her flat in Davies Street was too brief to allow time for reading and as soon as she was home, there was nearly always the usual rush to have a bath, change and go out. Or if she wasn't going out, there was even more of a rush to have a bath, change and start cooking for a dinner-party. Newspapers played a very small, insignificant part in her life, and none more so than the ones which came on sale in the evening.

On that particular evening, she had just finished changing and was embarking on the intricate task of make-up when an unexpected caller drifted into the flat and upset all her carefully-planned schedules.

"Just thought I'd drop in and see you. . . . Hope you don't mind. I say, I'm not in the way, am I?"

It had taken at least ten minutes to get rid of him, and even then he had wandered off leaving his tatty unwanted rag of an evening paper behind as if he had deliberately intended to leave his hall-mark on the room where he had wasted so much of her valuable time. Eve shoved the paper under the nearest cushion, whipped the empty glasses into the kitchen out of sight and sped back to add the final touches to her appearances.

And after all that, the man had to be late. All that panic and rush for nothing.

In the end she had time to spare; she took the evening paper from under the cushion and went into the kitchen absently to put it in the rubbish bin, but presently she hesitated. The paper would be useful to wrap up the bacon which had been slowly going bad since last weekend. Better do it now while she had a moment to spare or otherwise by the time next weekend came . . .

She opened the paper carelessly on the table and turned away towards the refrigerator.

A second later, the bacon forgotten, she turned back towards the table.

"Jon Towers, the Canadian property millionaire . . ."

Towers. Like . . . No, it couldn't be. It was imposible. She scrabbled to pick up the page, allowing the rest of the paper to slide on to the floor, not caring that her carefully-painted nails should graze against the surface of the table and scratch the varnish.

Jon without an H. Jon Towers. It was the same man.

A Canadian property millionaire . . . No, it couldn't be the same. But Jon had gone abroad following the aftermath of that weekend at Clougy. . . . Clougy! How funny that she should still remember the name. She could see it so clearly, too, the yellow house with white shutters which faced the sea, the green lawn of the garden, the hillside sloping down to the cove on either side of the house. The back of beyond, she had thought when she had first seen it, four miles from the nearest town, two miles from the main road, at the end of a track which led to nowhere. But at least she had never had to go there again. She had been there only once and that once had certainly been enough to last her a lifetime.

". . . staying in London. . . . English fiancée . . ."

Staying in London. One of the more well-known hotels, probably. It would be very simple to find out which one. . . .

If she wanted to find out. Which, of course, she didn't. Or did she?

24

Jon Towers, she was thinking as she stood there motionless, staring down at the blurred uncertain photograph. Joh Towers. Those eyes. You looked at those eyes and suddenly you forgot the pain in your back or the draught from the open door or a thousand and one other tiresome things which might be bothering you at that particular moment. You might loathe the piano and find all music tedious but as soon as he touched those piano keys you had to listen. He moved or laughed or made some trivial gesture with his hands and you had to watch him. A womanizer, she had decided when she had first met him, but then afterwards in their room that evening Max had said with that casual amused laugh, "Jon? Good God, didn't you notice? My dear girl, he's in love with his wife. Quaint, isn't it?"

His wife.

Eve put down the paper, and stooped to pick up the discarded pages. Her limbs were stiff and aching as if she had taken part in some violent exercise, and she felt cold for no apparent reason. After putting the paper automatically in the rubbish bin, she moved out of the kitchen and found herself re-entering the still, silent livingroom again.

So Jon Towers was back in London. He must have the hell of a nerve.

Perhaps, she thought idly, fingering the edge of the curtain as she stared out of the window, perhaps it would have been rather amusing to have met Jon again. Too bad he had probably forgotten she had ever existed and was now about to marry some girl she had never met. But it would have been interesting to see if those eyes and that powerful body could still infect her with that strange unnerving excitement even now after ten years, or whether this time she would have been able to look upon him with detachment. If the attraction were wholly sexual, it was possible she would not have been so impressed a second time . . . but there had been something else besides. She could remember trying to explain to Max and yet not being sure what she was trying to explain. "It's not just sex, Max. It's something else. It's not just sex."

And Max had smiled his favorite tired cynical smile and said, "No? Are you quite sure?"

Max Alexander.

Turning away from the window she went over to the telephone and after a moment's hesitation knelt down to take out a volume of the London telephone directory.

IV

Max Alexander was in bed. There was only one other place which he preferred to bed and that was behind the wheel of his racing car, but his doctors had advised him against racing that season and so he had more time to spend in bed. On that particular evening he had just awakened from a brief doze and was reaching out for a cigarette when the telephone bell rang far away on the other side of the mattress.

He picked up the receiver out of idle curiosity.

"Max Alexander speaking."

"Hullo, Max," said an unfamiliar woman's voice at the other end of the wire. "How are you?"

He hesitated, aware of a shaft of annoyance. Hell to these women with their ridiculous air of mystery and cool would-be call-girl voices which wouldn't even fool a two-year-old child. . . .

"This is Flaxman nine-eight-double-one," he said dryly. "I think you have the wrong number."

"You've got a short memory, Max," said the voice at

26

the other end of the line. "It wasn't really so long ago since Clougy, was it?"

After a long moment he managed to say politely into the white ivory receiver, "Since *when?*"

"Clougy, Max. Clougy. You surely haven't forgotten your friend Jon Towers, have you?"

The absurd thing was that he simply couldn't remember her name. He had a feeling it was biblical. Ruth, perhaps? Or Esther? Hell, there must be more female names in the Scriptures than that, but for the life of him he couldn't think of any more. It was nearly a quarter of a century since he had last opened a copy of the Bible.

"Oh, it's you," he said for lack of anything better to say. "How's the world treating you these days?"

What the devil was she telephoning for? After the affair at Clougy he had seen no more of her and they had gone their separate ways. Anyway, that was ten years ago. Ten years was an extremely long time.

". . . I've been living in a flat in Davies Street for the past two years," she was saying. "I'm working for a Piccadilly firm now. Diamond merchants. I work for the managing director."

As if he cared.

"You've seen the news about Jon, of course," she said carelessly before he could speak. "Today's evening paper."

"Jon?"

"You haven't seen the paper? He's back in London."

There was a silence. The world was suddenly reduced to a white ivory telephone receiver and a sickness below his heart which hurt his lungs.

"He's staying here for a few days. I gather he's here on some kind of business trip. I just wondered if you knew. Didn't he write and tell you he was coming?"

"We lost touch with each other when he went abroad,"

27

said Alexander abruptly and replaced the receiver without waiting for her next comment.

He was sweating, he noticed with surprise, and his lungs were still pumping the blood around his heart in a way which would have worried his doctors. Lying back on the pillows he tried to breathe more evenly and concentrate on the ceiling above him.

Really, women were quite extraordinary, always falling over themselves to be the first bearers of unexpected news. He supposed it gave them some peculiar thrill, some spurious touch of pleasure. This woman had obviously been reveling in her role of self-appointed newscaster.

"Jon Towers," he said aloud. "Jon Towers." It helped him to recall the past little by little, he decided. It was soothing and restful and helped him to view the situation from a disinterested, dispassionate point of view. He hadn't thought of Jon for a long time. How had he got on in Canada? And why should he have come back now after all those years? It had always seemed so obvious that he would never under any circumstances come back after his wife died. . . .

Alexander stiffened as he thought of Sophia's death. That had been a terrible business; even now he could remember the inquest, the doctors, the talks with the police as if it were yesterday. The jury had returned a verdict of accident in the end, although the possibility of suicide had also been discussed, and Jon had left the house after that, sold his business in Penzance and had been in Canada within two months.

Alexander shook a cigarette out of the packet by his bed and lit it slowly, watching the tip burn and smoulder as he pushed it into the orange flame. But his thoughts were quickening, gathering speed and clarity as the memories slipped back into his mind. Jon and he had

28

been at school together. To begin with they hadn't had much in common, but then Jon had become interested in motor-racing and they had started seeing each other in the holidays and staying at one another's houses. Jon had had an odd sort of home life. His mother had been an ex-debutante type, very snobbish, and he had spent most of his time quarreling with her. His parents had been divorced when he was seven. His father, who had apparently been very rich and extremely eccentric, had lived abroad after that and had spent most of his life making expeditions to remote islands in search of botanical phenomena, so that Jon had never seen him at all. There had been various other relations on the mother's side, but the only relation of his that Alexander had ever met had come from old Towers' side of the family. She had been a year younger than Jon and Alexander himself, and her name had been Marijohn.

He wasn't in the room at all now. He was far away in another world and there was sun sparkling on blue waters from a cloudless sky. Marijohn, he thought, and remembered how they had even called her that too. It had never been shortened to Mary. It had always been Marijohn, the first and last syllable both stressed exactly the same. Marijohn Towers.

When he had been older he had tried taking her out for a while as she was rather good-looking, but he might just as well have saved his energy because he had never got anywhere. There had been too many other men all with the same aim in view, and anyway she had seemed to prefer men much older than herself. Not that Alexander had minded; he had never even begun to understand what she was thinking, and although he could tolerate mysterious women in small doses he always became irritated if the air of mystery was completely impenetrable. . . . She had married a solicitor in the end. Nobody had known why. He had been a very ordinary sort of fellow, rather dull and desperately conventional. Michael, he had been called. Michael something-or-other. But they were divorced now anyway and Alexander didn't know what had happened to either of them since then.

But before Marijohn had married Michael, Jon had married Sophia. . . .

The cigarette smoke was hurting his lungs and suddenly he didn't want to think about the past any more. Sophia, astonishingly enough, had been a Greek waitress in a Soho café. Jon had been nineteen when he had met her and they had married soon afterwards—much to the disgust of his mother, naturally, and to the fury of his father who had immediately abandoned his latest expedition to fly back to England. There had been appalling rows on all sides and in the end the old man had cut Jon out of his will and returned to rejoin his expedition. Alexander gave a wry smile. Jon hadn't given a damn! He had borrowed a few thousand pounds from his mother, gone to the opposite end of England and had started up an estate agent's business down in Penzance, Cornwall. He had paid her back, of course. He had made a practice of buying up cottages in favorable parts of Cornwall, converting them and selling them at a profit. Cornwall had been at its height of popularity then, and it was easy enough for a man like Jon who had had capital and a head for money to earn enough to pay his way in the world. Anyway he hadn't been interested in big money at that particular time—all he had wanted had been his wife, a beautiful home in peaceful surroundings and his grand piano. He had got all three, of course. Jon had always got what he wanted.

The memories darkened suddenly, twisting and turning in his mind like revolving knives. Yes, he thought,

Jon had always got what he wanted. He wanted a woman and he had only to crook his little finger; he wanted money and it flowed gently into his bank account; he wanted you to be a friend for some reason and you became a friend. . . . Or did you? When he was no longer there, it was as if a spell had been lifted and you started to wonder why you had ever been friends with him. . . .

He thought of Jon's marriage again. There had only been one child, and he had been fat and rather plain and hadn't looked much like either of his parents. Alexander felt the memories quicken in his mind again; he was recalling the weekend parties at Clougy throughout the summer when the Towers' friends would drive down on Friday, sometimes doing the journey in a day, sometimes stopping Friday night en route and arriving on Saturday for lunch. It had been a long drive, but Jon and Sophia had entertained well and anyway the place had been a perfect retreat for any long weekend. . . . In a way it had been too much of a retreat, especially for Sophia who had lived all her life in busy crowded cities. There was no doubt that she had soon tired of that beautiful secluded house by the sea that Jon had loved so much, and towards the end of her life she had become very restless.

· He thought of Sophia then, the voluptuous indolence, the languid movements, the dreadful stifled boredom never far below the lush surface. Poor Sophia. It would have been better by far if she had stayed in her cosmopolitan restaurant instead of exchanging the teeming life of Soho for the remote serenity of that house by the sea.

He went on thinking, watching his cigarette burn, remembering the rocks beneath the cove where she had fallen. It would have been easy enough to fall, he had thought at the time. There had been a path, steps cut out

31

of the cliff, but it had been sandy and insecure after rain and although the cliff hadn't been very steep or very big the rocks below had been like a lot of jagged teeth before they had flattened out in terraces to the water's edge.

He stubbed out his cigarette, grinding the butt of ashes. It had been a beautiful spot below those cliffs. Jon had often walked out there with the child.

He could see it all so clearly now, that weekend he had been at Clougy for one of the gay parties which Sophia had loved so much. He had come down with Eve, and Michael had come down with Marijohn. There had been no one else, just the four of them with Jon, Sophia and the child. Jon had invited another couple as well but they hadn't been able to come at the last minute so there had only been four visitors at Clougy that weekend.

He saw Clougy then in his mind's eye, the old farmhouse that Jon had converted, a couple of hundred yards from the sea. There had been yellow walls and white shutters. It had been an unusual, striking place. Afterwards when it was all over, he had thought Jon would sell his home, but he had not. Jon had sold his business in Penzance, but he had never sold Clougy. He had given it all to Marijohn.

V

As soon as Michael Rivers reached his home that evening he took his car from the garage and started on the long journey south from his flat in Westminster to the remote house forty miles away in Surrey. At Guildford he paused to eat a snack supper at one of the pubs, and then he set off again towards Hindhead and the Devil's

Punchbowl. It was just after seven o'clock when he reached Anselm's Cross, and the July sun was flaming in the sky beyond the pine trees of the surrounding hills.

He was received with surprise, doubt and more than a hint of disapproval. Visitors were not allowed on Tuesday as a general rule; the Mother Superior was very particular about it. However, if it was urgent, it was always possible for an exception to be made.

"You are expected, of course?"

"No," said Rivers, "but I think she'll see me."

"One moment, please," said the woman abruptly and left the room in a swirl of black skirts and black veil.

He waited about a quarter of an hour in that bare little room until he thought his patience must surely snap and then at last the woman returned, her lips thin with disapproval. "This way, please."

He followed her down long corridors, the familiar silence suffocating him. For a moment he tried to imagine what it would be like to live in such a place, cut off from the world, imprisoned with one's thoughts for hours on end, but his mind only recoiled from the thought and the sweat of horror started to prickle beneath his skin. To counteract the nightmarish twists of his imagination he forced himself to think of his life as it was at that moment, the weekdays crammed with his work at the office, his evenings spent at his club playing bridge or perhaps entertaining clients, the weekends filled with golf and the long hours in the open air. There was never any time to sit and think. It was better that way. Once long ago he had enjoyed solitude from time to time, but now he longed only for his mind to be absorbed with other people and activities which would keep any possibility of solitude far beyond his reach.

The nun opened a door. When he passed across the threshold, she closed the door again behind him and he heard the soft purposeful tread of her shoes as she walked briskly away again down the corridor.

"Michael!" said Marijohn with a smile. "What a lovely surprise!"

She stood up, moving across the floor towards him, and as she reached him the sun slanted through the window on to her beautiful hair. There was a tightness in his throat suddenly, an ache behind the eyes, and he stood helplessly before her, unable to speak, unable to move, almost unable to see.

"Dear Michael," he heard her say gently. "Come and sit down and tell me what it's all about. Is it bad news? You would hardly have driven all the way down here after a hard day's work otherwise."

She had sensed his distress, but not the reason for it. He managed to tighten his self-control as she turned to lead the way over to the two chairs, one on either side of the table, and the next moment he was sitting down opposite her and fumbling for his cigarette case.

"Mind if I smoke?" he mumbled, his eyes on the table.

"Not a bit. Can you spare one for me?"

He looked up in surprise, and she smiled at his expression. "I'm not a nun," she reminded him. "I'm not even a novice. I'm merely 'in retreat'. "

"Of course," he said clumsily. "I always seem to forget that." He offered her a cigarette. She still wore the wedding ring, he noticed, and her fingers as she accepted the cigarette were long and slim, just as he remembered.

"Your hair's grayer, Michael," she said. "I suppose you're still working too hard at the office." And then, as she inhaled from the cigarette a moment later: "How strange it tastes! Most odd. Like some rare poison bringing a slow soporific death. . . . How long is it since you last came, Michael? Six months?"

"Seven. I came last Christmas."

"Of course! I remember now. Have you still got the same flat? Westminster, wasn't it? It's funny but I simply can't picture you in Westminster at all. You ought to marry again, Michael, and live in some splendid suburb like—like Richmond or Roehampton or somewhere." She blew smoke reflectively at the ceiling. "How are all your friends? Have you seen Camilla again? I remember you said you'd met her at some party last Christmas."

His self-possession was returning at last. He felt a shaft of gratitude towards her for talking until he felt better and then for giving him the precise opening he needed. It was almost as if she had known. . . . But no, that was impossible. She couldn't possibly have known."

"No," he said. "I haven't seen Camilla again."

"Or Justin?"

She must know. His scalp started to prickle because the knowledge was so uncanny.

"No, you wouldn't have seen Justin," she said answering her own question before he could reply. She spoke more slowly, he noticed, and her eyes were turned towards the window, focused on some remote object which he could not see. "I think I understand," she said at last. "You must have come to talk to me about Jon."

The still silence was all around them now, a huge tide of noiselessness which engulfed them completely. He tried to imagine that he was in his office and she was merely another client with whom he had to discuss business, but although he tried to speak the words refused to come.

"He's come back."

She was looking at him directly for the first time, and her eyes were very steady, willing him to speak.

"Yes?"

Another long motionless silence. She was looking at her hands now, and the long lashes seemed to shadow her face and give it the strange veiled look he had come to dread once long ago.

"Where is he?"

"In London."

"With Camilla?"

"No, at the Mayfair Hotel." The simple routine of question and answer reminded him of countless interviews with clients, and suddenly it seemed easier to talk. "It was in the evening paper," he said. "They called him a Canadian property millionaire, which seemed rather unlikely, but it was definitely Jon because there was a photograph and of course, being the society page, the writer had to mention Camilla. The name of the hotel wasn't stated but I rang up the major hotels until I found the right one—it didn't take very long, less than ten minutes. I didn't think he would be staying with Camilla because when I last met her she said she had competely lost touch with him and didn't even know his Canadian address."

"I see." A pause. "Did the paper say anything else?"

"Yes," he said, "it did. It said he was engaged to an English girl and planned to marry shortly."

She looked out of the window at the evening light and the clear blue sky far away. Presently she smiled. "I'm glad," she said, glancing back at him so that she was smiling straight into his eyes. "That's wonderful news. I hope he'll be very happy."

He was the first to look away, and as he stared down at the hard, plain, wooden surface of the table he had a sudden longing to escape from this appalling silence and race back through the twilight to the garish noise of London. "Would you like me to—" he heard himself mumbling but she interrupted him.

"No," she said, "there's no need for you to see him on my behalf. It was kind of you to come all this way to

36

see me tonight, but there's nothing more you can do now."

"If—if ever you need anything—want any help . . ."

"I know," she said. "I'm very grateful, Michael."

He made his escape soon after that. She held out her hand to him as he said good-bye but that would have made the parting too formal and remote so he pretended not to see it. And then, minutes later, he was switching on the engine of his car and turning the knob of the little radio up to the maximum volume before setting off on his return journey to London.

VI

After he had gone, Marijohn sat for a long while at the wooden table and watched the night fall. When it was quite dark, she knelt down by the bed and prayed.

At eleven o'clock she undressed to go to bed, but an hour later she was still awake and the moonlight was beginning to slant through the little window and cast long, elegant shadows on the bare walls.

She sat up, listening. Her mind was opening again, a trick she thought she had forgotten long ago, and after a while she went over to the window and opened it as if the cool night air would help her struggle to interpret and understand. Outside was the quiet closed courtyard, even more quiet and closed than her room, but now instead of soothing her with its peace the effect reversed itself stealthily so that she felt her head seem to expand and the breath choke in her throat, making her want to scream. She ran to the door and opened it, her lungs gasping, the sweat breaking out all over her body, but outside was merely the quiet, closed corridor, suffocating her with its peace. She started to run, her bare feet

37

making no sound on the stone floor, and suddenly she was running along the cliffs by tht blue sparkling Cornish sea, running and running towards a house with yellow walls and white shutters, and the open air was all around her and she was free.

The scene blurred in her mind. She was in the garden of the old house in Surrey and there was a rose growing in a bed nearby. She plucked it out, tearing the petals to shreds, and then suddenly her mind was opening again and she was frightened. Nobody, she thought, nobody who hasn't this other sense can ever understand how frightening it is. They could never conceive what it means. They can imagine their bodies being scarred or hurt by some ordinary physical force but they can never imagine the pain in the mind, the dark struggles to understand, the knowledge that your mind doesn't belong to yourself alone. . . .

She knelt down, trying to pray, but her prayer was lost in the storm and she could only kneel and listen to her mind.

And when the dawn came at last she went to the Mother Superior to tell her that she would be leaving the house that day and did not know when she would ever return.

Two

I

THE HOTEL staff at the reception desk were unable to trace the anonymous call.

"But you must," said Jon. "It's very important. You must."

The man behind the desk said courteously that he regretted that it was quite impossible. It was a local call made from a public telephone booth but the automatic dialing system precluded any possibility of finding out any further information.

"Was it a man or a woman?"

"I'm afraid I don't remember, sir."

"But you must!" said Jon. "Surely you remember. The call only came through a minute ago."

"But sir—" The man felt himself stammering. "You see—"

"What did he say? Was it a deep voice? Did he have any accent?"

"No, sir. At least it was difficult to tell because—"

"Why?"

"Well, it was little more than a whisper, sir. Very faint. He just asked for you. 'Mr. Towers please,' he said and I said, 'Mr. Jon Towers?' and when he didn't answer I said, 'One moment, please' and connected the lines." He stopped.

Jon said nothing. Then after a moment, he shrugged his shoulders abruptly and turned aside, crossing the hall and reception lounge to the bar, while the man behind the desk wiped his forehead, muttered something to his companion and sat down automatically on the nearest available chair.

In the bar Jon ordered a double Scotch on the rocks. There was a sprinkling of people in the room but it was easy enough to find a seat at a comfortable distance from the nearest group, and when he sat down he lit a cigarette before starting his drink. After a while he became conscious of one definite need dominating the mass of confused thoughts in his mind, and on finishing his drink he stubbed out his cigarette and returned to his room to make a phone call.

A stranger's voice answered.

Hell, thought Jon in a blaze of frustration she's moved or remarried or both and I'll have to waste time being a bloody private detective trying to discover where she is."

"Mrs. Rivington, please," he said abruptly to the unknown voice at the other end of the wire.

"I think you have the wrong number. This is—"

"Is that Forty-one Halkin Street?"

"Yes, but—"

"Then she's moved," said Jon wearily and added, "Thank you," before slamming down the receiver.

He sat and thought for a moment. Lawrence, the family lawyer, would probably know where she was. Lawrence wouldn't have moved in ten years either; he would be seventy-five now, firmly embedded in his little Georgian house at Richmond with his crusty housekeeper who probably still wore starched collars and cuffs.

Ten minutes later he was speaking to a deep mellifluous voice which pronounced each syllable with meticulous care.

"Lawrence, I'm trying to get in touch with my mother.

Can you give me her address? I've just rung Halkin Street but I gather she's moved from there and it occurred to me that you would probably be able to tell me what's been happening while I've been abroad."

Lawrence talked for thirty seconds until Jon could stand it no longer.

"You mean she moved about five years ago after her second husband died and is now living at Five, Consett Mews?"

"Precisely. In fact—"

"I see. Now Lawrence, there's just one other thing. I'm extremely anxious to trace my cousin Marijohn—I was planning to phone my mother and ask her, but I suppose I may as well ask you now I'm speaking to you. Have you any idea where she is?"

The old man pondered over the question.

"You mean," said John after ten seconds, "you don't know."

"Well, in actual fact, to be completely honest, no I don't. Couldn't say. Rivers could tell you, of course. Nice chap, young Rivers. Sorry their marriage wasn't a success. . . . You knew about the divorce, I suppose?"

There was a silence in the softly-lit room. Beyond the window far-away traffic crawled up Berkeley Street, clockwork toys moving slowly through a model town.

"The divorce was—let me see . . . six years ago? Five? My memory's not so accurate as it used to be. . . . Rivers was awfully cut up about it—met him at the Law Society just about the time the divorce was coming up for hearing and he looked damn ill, poor fellow. No trouble with the divorce, though. Simple undefended desertion—took about ten minutes and the judge was pretty decent about it. Marijohn wasn't in court, of course. No need for her to be there when she wasn't defending the petition. . . . Are you still there, Jon?"

"Yes," said Jon, "I'm still here." And in his mind his voice was saying Marijohn, Marijohn, Marijohn over and over again, and the room was suddenly dark with grief.

Lawrence wandered on inconsequentially, reviewing the past ten years with the reminiscing nostalgia of the very old. He seemed surprised when Jon suddenly terminated the conversation, but managed to collect himself sufficiently to invite Jon to his home for dinner later that week.

"I'm sorry, Lawrence, but I'm afraid that won't be possible at the moment. I'll phone you later, if I may, and perhaps we can arrange something then."

After he had replaced the receiver he slumped on to the bed and buried his face in the pillow for a moment. The white linen was cool against his cheek, and he remembered how he had loved the touch of linen years ago when they had first used the sheets and pillowcases which had been given to them as wedding presents. In a sudden twist of memory he could see the double bed in their room at Clougy, the white sheets crisp and inviting, Sophia's dark hair tumbling over the pillows, her naked body full and rich and warm.. . . .

He sat up, moved into the bathroom and then walked back into the bedroom to the window in a restless fever of movement. Find Marijohn, said the voice at the back of his brain. You have to find Marijohn. You can't go to Michael Rivers so you must go to your mother instead. Best to call Consett Mews, and then maybe you can see Justin at the same time and arrange to have a talk with him. You must see Justin.

But that phone call. I have to find out who made that phone call. And most important of all, I must find Marijohn. . . .

He went out, hailing a taxi at the curb, and giving his mother's address to the driver before slumping on to the back seat. The journey didn't take long. John sat and watched the dark trees of the park flash into the brilliant vortex of Knightsbridge, and then the cab turned off beyond Harrods before twisting into Consett Mews two minutes later. He got out, gave the man a ten shilling note and decided not to bother to wait for change. It was dark in the mews; the only light came from an old-fashioned lamp set on a corner some yards away, and there was no light on over the door marked Five. Very slowly he crossed the cobbles and pushed the bell hard and long with the index finger of his right hand.

Perhaps Justin will come to the door, he thought. For the hundredth time he tried to imagine what Justin would look like, but he could only see the little boy with the short fat legs and plump body, and suddenly he was back in the past again with the small trusting hand tightly clasping his own throughout the walks along the cliff path to Clougy. . . .

The door opened. Facing him on the threshold was a woman in a maid's uniform whose face he did not know.

"Good evening," said Jon. "Is Mrs. Rivington in?"

The maid hesitated uncertainly. And then a woman's voice said, "Who is it?" and the next moment as Jon stepped across the threshold, Camilla came out into the hall.

There was a tightness in Jon's chest suddenly, an ache of love in his throat, but the past rose up in a great smothering mist and he was left only with his familiar detachment. She had never cared. She had always been too occupied in finding lovers and husbands, too busy trekking the weary social rounds of cocktail parties and grand occasions, too intent on hiring nursemaids to do her work for her or making arrangements to send him off to boarding school a year early so that he would no longer be in the way. He accepted her attitude and had adjusted himself to it. There was no longer any pain now, least of all after ten years away from her.

"Hullo," he said, hoping she wouldn't cry or make some emotional scene to demonstrate a depth of love which did not exist. "I thought I'd just call in and see you. No doubt you saw in the paper that I was in London."

"Jon . . ." She took him in her arms, and as he kissed her on the cheek he knew she was crying.

So there was to be the familiar emotional scene after all. It would be like the time she had sent him to boarding school at the age of seven and had then cried when the time had come for him to go. He had never forgiven her for crying, for the hypocrisy of assuming a grief which she could not possibly have felt in the circumstances, and now it seemed that the hypocrisy was about to begin all over again.

He stepped backwards away from her and smiled into her eyes. "Why," he said slowly, "I don't believe you've changed at all. . . . Where's Justin? Is he here?"

Her expression changed almost imperceptibly; she turned to lead the way back into the drawing-room. "No, he's not. He went out after dinner, and said he wouldn't be in until about eleven. . . . Why didn't you phone and let us know you intended to see us? I didn't expect a letter, of course—that would have been too much to hope for—but if you'd phoned—"

"I didn't know whether I was going to have time to come tonight."

They were in the drawing-room. He recognized the familiar pictures, the oak cabinet, the pale willow-pattern china.

"How long are you here for?" she said quickly. "Is it a business trip?"

"In a way," said Jon abruptly. "I'm also here to get married. My fiancée is traveling over from Toronto in ten days' time and we're getting married quietly as soon as possible."

"Oh?" she said, and he heard the hard edge to her voice and knew the expression in her eyes would be hard too. "Am I invited to the wedding? Or is it to be such a quiet affair that not even the bridegroom's mother is invited?"

"You may come if you wish." He took a cigarette from the box on the table and lit it with his own lighter. "But we want it to be quiet. Sarah's parents had the idea of throwing a big society wedding in Canada, but that was more than I could stand and certainly the last thing Sarah wanted, so we decided to have the wedding in London. Her parents will fly over from Canada and there'll be one or two of her friends there as well, but no one else."

"I see," said his mother. "How interesting. And have you told her all about your marriage to Sophia?"

There was a pause. He looked at her hard and had the satisfaction of seeing the color suffuse her neck and creep upwards into her face. After a moment he said to her carefully, "Did you phone the Mayfair Hotel this evening?"

"Did I—" She was puzzled. He saw her eyes cloud in bewilderment. "No, I didn't know you were staying at the Mayfair," she said at last. "I made no attempt to phone you. . . . Why do you ask?"

"Nothing." He inhaled from his cigarette, and glanced at a new china figurine on the dresser. "How are Michael and Marijohn these days?" he asked casually after a moment.

"They're divorced."

"Really?" His voice was vaguely surprised. "Why was that?"

"She wouldn't live with him any more. I've no doubt there were various affairs too. He divorced her for desertion in the end."

He gave a slight shrug of the shoulders as if in comment, and knew, without looking at her, that she wanted to say something spiteful. Before she could speak he asked, "Where's Marijohn now?"

A pause.

"Why?"

He looked at her directly. "Why not? I want to see her."

"I see," she said. "That was why you came to England I suppose. And why you called here tonight. I'm sure you wouldn't have bothered otherwise."

Oh God, thought Jon wearily. More histrionic scenes.

"Well, you've wasted your time coming here in that case," she said tightly. "I've no idea where she is, and I don't give a damn either. Michael's the only one who keeps in touch with her."

"Where does he live now?"

"Westminster," said Camilla, her voice clear and hard. "Sixteen, Grays Court. You surely don't want to go and see Michael, do you, darling?"

Jon leant forward, flicked ash into a tray and stood up with the cigarette still burning between his fingers.

"You're not going, are you, for heaven's sake? You've only just arrived!"

"I'll come again some time. I'm very rushed at the moment." He was already moving out into the hall, but as she followed him he paused with one hand on the front door latch and turned to face her.

She stopped.

He smiled.

"Jon," she said suddenly, all anger gone. "Jon darling—"

"Ask Justin to phone me when he comes in, would you?" he said, kissing her good-bye and holding her close to him for a moment. "Don't forget. I want to have a word with him tonight."

She moved away from him and he withdrew his arms and opened the front door.

"You don't want to see him, do you?" he heard her say, and he mistook the fear in her voice for sarcasm. "I didn't think you would be sufficiently interested."

He turned abruptly and stepped out into the dark street. "Of course I want to see him," he said over his shoulder. "Didn't you guess? Justin was the main reason why I decided to come back."

II

Michael Rivers was out. Jon rang the bell of the flat three times and then rattled the door handle in frustration, but as he turned to walk away down the stairs he was conscious of a feeling of relief. He had not wanted to see Rivers again.

He turned the corner of the stairs and began to walk slowly down the last flight into the main entrance hall, but just as he reached the last step the front door swung open. The next moment a man had crossed the threshold and was pausing to close the door again behind him.

It was dark in the hall. Jon was in shadow, motionless, almost holding his breath, and then as the man turned, one hand still on the latch, he knew that the man was Michael Rivers.

"Who's that?" said the man sharply.

"Jon Towers." He had decided on the journey to

47

Westminster that it would be futile to waste time making polite conversation or pretending that ten years had made any difference to the situation. "Forgive me for calling on you like this," he said directly, moving out of the shadows into the dim evening dusk. "But I wanted your help. I have to trace Marijohn urgently and no one except you seems to know where she is."

He was nearer Rivers now, but he still could not see him properly. The man had not moved at all, and the odd half-light was such that Jon could not see the expression in his eyes. He was aware of a sharp pang of uneasiness, a violent twist of memory which was so vivid that it hurt, and then an inexplicable wave of compassion.

"I'm sorry things didn't work out," he said suddenly. "It must have been hard."

The fingers on the latch slowly loosened their grip; Rivers turned away from the door and paused by the table to examine the second post which lay waiting there for the occupants of the house.

"I'm afraid I can't tell you where she is."

"But you must," said Jon. "I have to see her. You must."

The man's back was to him, his figure still and implacable.

"Please," said Jon, who loathed having to beg from anyone. "It's very important. Please tell me."

The man picked up an envelope and started to open it.

"Is she in London?"

It was a bill. He put it back neatly in the envelope and turned towards the stairs.

"Look, Michael—"

"Go to hell."

"Where is she?"

"Get out of my—"

"You've got to tell me. Don't be so bloody stupid! This is urgent. You must tell me."

The man wrenched himself free of Jon's grip and started up the stairs. When Jon moved swiftly after him he swung round and for the first time Jon saw the expression in his eyes.

"You've caused too much trouble in your life, Jon Towers, and you've caused more than enough trouble for Marijohn. If you think I'm fool enough to tell you where she is, you're crazy. You've come to the very last person on Earth who would ever tell you, and it so happens—fortunately for Marijohn—that I'm the only person who knows where she is. Now get the hell out of here before I lose my temper and call the police."

The words were still and soft, the voice almost a whisper in the silent hall. Jon stepped back and paused.

"So it was you who called me this evening."

Rivers stared at him. "Called you?"

"Called me on the phone. I had an anonymous phone call welcoming me back to England and the welcome wasn't particularly warm. I thought it might be you."

Rivers still stared. Then he turned away as if in disgust. "I don't know what you're talking about," Jon heard him say as he started to mount the stairs again. "I'm a solicitor, not a crank who makes anonymous phone calls."

The stairs creaked; he turned the corner and Jon was alone suddenly with his thoughts in the dim silent hall.

He went out, finding his way to Parliament Square and walking past Big Ben to the Embankment. Traffic roared in his ears, lights blazed, diesel oil choked his lungs. He walked rapidly, trying to expel all the fury and frustration and fear from his body by a burst of physical energy, and then suddenly he knew no physical movement was going to soothe the turmoil in his mind and

49

he stopped in exhaustion, leaning against the parapet to stare down into the dark waters of the Thames.

Marijohn, said his brain over and over again, each thought pattern harsh with anxiety and jagged with distress. Marijohn, Marijohn, Marijohn . . .

If only he could find out who had made the phone call. Even though he had for a moment suspected his mother he was certain she wasn't responsible. The person who had made that call must have been at Clougy during that last terrible weekend, and although his mother might have guessed what had happened with the help of her own special knowledge she would never think that he . . .

Better not to put it into words. Words were irrevocable forms of expression, terrible in their finality.

So it wasn't his mother. And he was almost certain it wasn't Michael Rivers. Almost . . . And of course it wasn't Marijohn. So that left Max and the girl Max had brought down from London that weekend, the tall, rather disdainful blonde called Eve. Poor Max, getting himself in such a muddle, trying to fool himself that he knew everything there was to know about women, constantly striving to be a second-rate Don Juan, when the only person he ever fooled was himself. . . . It was painfully obvious that the only reason why women found him attractive was because he led the social life of the motor racing set and had enough money to lead it in lavish style.

Jon went into Charing Cross Underground Station and shut himself in a phone booth.

It would be Eve, of course. Women often made anonymous phone calls. But what did she know and how much? Perhaps it was her idea of a practical joke and she knew nothing at all. Perhaps it was merely the first step in some plan to blackmail him, and in that case . . .

50

His thoughts spun round dizzily as he found the number in the book and picked up the receiver to dial.

He glanced at his watch as the line began to purr. It was getting late. Whatever happened he mustn't forget to phone Sarah at midnight. . . . Midnight in London, six o'clock in Toronto. Sarah would be playing the piano when the call came through and when the bell rang she would push the lock of dark hair from her forehead and run from the music room to the telephone. . . .

The line clicked. "Flaxman nine-eight-double-one," said a man's voice abruptly at the other end.

The picture of Sarah died.

"Max?"

A pause. Then! "Speaking."

He suddenly found it difficult to go on. In the end he merely said, "This is Jon, Max. Thanks for the welcoming phone call this evening—how did you know I was in town?"

The silence that followed was embarrassingly long. Then: "I'm sorry," said Max Alexander. "I hope I don't sound too dense but I'm completely at sea. John—"

"Towers."

"Jon Towers! Good God, what a sensation! I thought it must be you but as I know about two dozen people called John I thought I'd better make quite sure who I was talking to. . . . What's all this about a welcoming phone call?"

"Didn't you ring me up at the hotel earlier this evening and welcome me home?"

"My dear chap, I didn't even know you were in London until somebody rang up and told me you'd been mentioned in the evening paper—"

"Who?"

"What?"

"Who rang you up?"

"Well, curiously enough it was that girl I brought down to Clougy with me the weekend when—"

"Eve?"

"Eve! Why, of course! Eve Robertson. I'd forgotten her name for a moment, but you're quite right. It was Eve."

"Where does she live now?"

"Well, as a matter of fact, I think she said she was living in Davies Street. She said she worked in Piccadilly for a firm of diamond merchants. Why on earth do you want to know? I lost touch with her years ago, almost immediately after that weekend at Clougy."

"Then why the hell did she phone you this evening?"

"God knows . . . Look, Jon, what's all this about? What are you trying to—"

"It's nothing," said Jon. "Never mind, Max—forget it; it doesn't matter. Look, perhaps I can see you sometime within the next few days? It's a long while since we last met and ten years is time enough to be able to bury whatever happened between us. Have dinner with me tomorrow night at the Hawaii at nine and tell me all you've been doing with yourself during the last ten years. . . . Are you married, by the way? Or are you still fighting for your independence?"

"No," said Alexander slowly. "I've never married."

"Then let's have dinner by ourselves tomorrow. No women. My days of being a widower are numbered and I'm beginning to appreciate stag-parties again. Did you see my engagement mentioned in the paper tonight, by the way? I met an English girl in Toronto earlier this year and decided I was sick of housekeepers, paid and unpaid, and tired of all American and Canadian women. . . . You must meet Sarah when she comes to England."

52

"Yes," said Alexander. "I should like to." And then his voice added idly without warning: "Is she like Sophia?"

The telephone booth was a tight constricting cell clouded with a white mist of rage. "Yes," said Jon rapidly. "Physically she's very like her indeed. If you want to alter the dinner arrangements for tomorrow night, Max, phone me at the hotel tomorrow and if I'm not there, you can leave a message."

When he put the receiver back into the cradle he leant against the door for a moment and pressed his cheek against the glass pane. He felt drained of energy suddenly, emotionally exhausted.

And still he was no nearer finding Marijohn. . . .

But at least it seemed probable that Eve was responsible for the anonymous phone call. And at least he now knew where she lived and what her surname was.

Wrenching the receiver from the hook again he started dialing to contact the operator in charge of Directory Inquiries.

III

Eve was furious. It was a long time since she had been let down by someone who had promised to give her an entertaining evening, and an even longer time since she had made a date with a man who had simply failed to turn up as he had promised. To add to her feeling of frustration and anger, the phone call to Max Alexander, which should have been so amusing, had been a failure, and after Alexander had slammed down the receiver in the middle of their conversation she had been left only with a great sense of anticlimax and depression.

Hell to Max Alexander. Hell to all men everywhere. Hell to everyone and everything.

The phone call came just as she was toying with her third drink and wondering whom she could ring up next in order to stave off the boredom of the long, empty evening ahead of her.

She picked up the receiver quickly, almost spilling the liquid from her glass.

"Hullo?"

"Eve?"

A man's voice, hard and taut. She sat up a little, the glass forgotten.

"Speaking," she said with interest. "Who's this?"

There was a pause. And then after a moment the hard voice said abruptly, "Eve, this is Jon Towers."

The glass tipped, jerked off balance by the reflex of her wrist and hand. It toppled on to the carpet, the liquid splashing in a dark pool upon the floor and all she could do was sit on the edge of the chair and watch the stain as it widened and deepened before her eyes.

"Why, hullo, Jon," she heard herself say, her voice absurdly cool and even. "I saw you were back in London. How did you know where I was?"

"I've just been talking to Max Alexander."

Thoughts were flickering back and forth across her mind in confused uncertain patterns. As she waited, baffled and intrigued, for him to make the next move she was again aware of the old memory of his personal magnetism and was conscious that his voice made the memory unexpectedly vivid.

"Are you busy?" he said suddenly. "Can I see you?"

"That would be nice," she said as soon as she was capable of speech. "Thank you very much."

"Tonight?"

"Yes . . . Yes, I could manage tonight."

"Could you meet me at the Mayfair Hotel in quarter of an hour?"

"Easily. It's just round the corner from where I live."

"I'll meet you in the lobby," he said. "Don't bother to ask for me at the reception desk." And then the next moment he was gone and the dead line was merely a dull expressionless murmur in her ear.

IV

After he had replaced the receiver, Jon left the station, walked up to Trafalfar Square and on towards Piccadilly. As he walked he started to worry about Sarah. Perhaps he could clear up this trouble with Eve during the ten days before Sarah arrived, but if not he would seriously have to consider inventing some reason for asking Sarah to delay her arrival. Whatever happened, Sarah must never discover the events which had taken place at Clougy ten years ago. He thought of Sarah for a moment, remembering her clear unsophisticated view of life and the naïve trust which he loved so much. She would never, never be able to understand, and in failing to understand she would be destroyed; the knowledge would tear away the foundations of her secure, stable world and once her world had collapsed she would be exposed to the great flaming beacon of reality with nothing to shield her from the flames.

He walked down Piccadilly to Berkeley Street, and still the traffic roared in his ears and pedestrians thronged the pavements. He was conscious of loneliness again, and the bleakness of the emotion was at once accentuated by his worries. It would have been different in Canada. There he could have absorbed himself in his work or played the piano until the mood passed, but here there was nothing except the conventional ways of finding comfort in a foreign city. And he hated the adolescent futility of getting drunk and would have despised himself for having a woman within days of his coming marriage. It would have meant nothing, of course, but he would still have felt ashamed afterwards, full of guilt because he had done something which would hurt Sarah if she knew. Sarah wouldn't understand that the act with an unknown woman meant nothing and less than nothing, and if she ever found out, her eyes would be full of grief and bewilderment and pain. . . .

He couldn't bear the thought of hurting Sarah.

But the loneliness was hard to bear too.

If only he could find Marijohn. There must be some way of finding her. He would advertise. Surely someone knew where she was. . . .

His thoughts swam and veered in steep sharp patterns, and then he had reached the Ritz and was turning off into Berkeley Street. Ten yards down the road he paused listening, but there was nothing, only a sense of unrest and distress which was too vague to be identified. He walked on slowly, and two minutes later was entering the lobby of the hotel.

As he crossed the floor to the desk to ask for his key, he was conscious of someone watching him. With the key in his hand a moment later he swung round to look at the occupants of the open lounge directly behind him, and as he moved, the tall blonde with the faintly disdainful expression stubbed out her cigarette and looked across at him with a slight, cool smile.

He recognized her at once. He had never had any difficulty in remembering faces, and suddenly he was back at Clougy long ago and listening to Sophia say

56

languidly, "I wonder who on earth Max will turn up with this time?"

And Max had arrived an hour later in a hot-rod open Bentley with this elegant, very fastidious blonde on the front seat beside him.

Jon slipped the key of his room into his pocket and crossed the lobby towards her.

"Well, well," she said wryly when he was near enough. "It's been a long time."

"A very long time." He stood before her casually, his hands in his pockets, the fingers of his right hand playing with the key to his room. Presently he said, "After I'd spoken to Max on the phone this evening, I realized I should get in touch with you."

She raised her eyebrows a fraction, almost as if she didn't understand him. It was cleverly done, he thought. "Just because I phone Max out of interest and tell him you're back in town," she said, "and just because Max later tells you that I phoned him, why does it automatically follow that you should get in touch with me?"

The lobby was sprinkled with people; there was one group only a few feet away from them seated on the leather chairs of the open lounge.

"If we're going to talk," he said, "you'd better come upstairs. There's not enough privacy here."

She still looked slightly bewildered, but now the bewilderment was mingled with a cautious tinge of pleasure, as if events had taken an unexpected but not unwelcome turn. "Fine," she said, her smile still wary but slightly less cool as she rose to her feet to stand beside him. "Lead the way."

They crossed the wide lobby to the elevator, the girl walking with a quick smooth grace which she had acquired since he had last seen her. Her mouth was slim beneath pale lipstick, the lashes of her beautiful eyes too long and dark to be entirely natural, her fair hair swept upwards simply in a soft, full curve.

On entering the elevator he was able to look at her more closely, but as he glanced across towards her he knew she was aware of his scrutiny and he turned aside abruptly.

"Six," he said to the elevator operator.

"Yes, sir."

The lift drifted upwards lazily. Canned music was playing softly from some small, insidious loudspeaker concealed beneath the control panel. Jon was reminded of Canada suddenly; ceaseless background music was one of the transatlantic traits which he had found most difficult to endure when he had arrived from England long ago, and even now after ten years he still noticed it with a sense of irritation.

"Six, sir," said the man as the doors opened.

Jon led the way down the corridor to his room, unlocked the door and walked in.

The girl shrugged off her coat.

"Cigarette?" said Jon shortly, turning away to take a fresh packet of cigarettes from a drawer by the bed.

"Thanks." He could feel her watching him. While he was giving her the cigarette and offering her a light he tried to analyze her expression, but it was difficult. There was a hint of curiosity in her eyes, a glimpse of ironic amusement in the slight curve of her smile, a trace of tension in her stillness as if her composure were not as effortless as it appeared to be. Some element in her manner puzzled him, and in an instinctive attempt to prolong the opening conversation and give himself more time to decide upon the best method of handling the situation, he said idly, "You don't seem to have changed much since that weekend at Clougy."

"No?" she said wryly. "I hope I have. I was very young when I went to Clougy, and very stupid."

"I don't see what was so young and stupid about wanting to marry Max. Most women would prefer to marry rich men, and there's always a certain glamor attached to anyone in the motor racing set."

"I was young and stupid not to realize that Max—and a hell of a lot of other men—just aren't the marrying kind."

"Why go to the altar when you can get exactly what you want by a lie in a hotel register?" He flung himself into a chair opposite her and gestured to her to sit down. "Some women have so little to offer on a long-term basis."

"And most men aren't interested in long-term planning."

He smiled suddenly, standing up in a quick, lithe movement and moving over to the window, his hands deep in his pockets. "Marriage is on a long-term basis," he said. "Until the parties decide to get divorced." He flung himself down in the chair again with a laugh, and as he felt her eyes watching him in fascination he wondered for the hundredth time in his life why women found his restlessness attractive.

"I should like to meet your new fiancée," she said unexpectedly, "just out of interest."

"You wouldn't like her."

"Why? Is she like Sophia?"

"Utterly different." He started to caress the arm of the chair idly, smoothing the material with strong movements of his fingers. "You must have hated Sophia that weekend," he said at last, not looking at her. "If I hadn't been so involved in my own troubles I might have found the time to feel sorry for you." He paused.

Then: "Max did you a bad turn by taking you down to Clougy."

She shrugged. "It's all in the past now."

"Is it?"

A silence. "What do you mean?"

"When you called me on the phone this evening it seemed you wanted to revive the past."

She stared at him.

"Didn't you call me this evening?"

She still stared. He leaned forward, stubbed out his cigarette and was beside her on the bed before she had time to draw breath.

"Give me your cigarette."

She handed it to him without a word and he crushed the butt to ashes.

"Now," he said, not touching her but close enough to show her he would and could if she were obstinate. "Just what the hell do you think you're playing at?"

She smiled uncertainly, a faint fleeting smile, and pushed back a strand of hair from her forehead as if she were trying to decide what to say and finding it difficult. He felt his irritation grow, his patience fade, and he had to hold himself tightly in control to stem the rising ride of anger within him.

Something in his eyes must have given him away; she stopped, her fingers still touching her hair, her body motionless, and as she looked at him he was suddenly seized with a violent longing to shake her by the shoulders and wrench the truth from behind the cool, composed expression.

"Damn you," he said quietly to the woman. "Damn you."

There was a noise. He stopped. The noise was a bell, hideous and insistent, a jet of ice across the fire of his anger. Pushing the woman aside, he leant across and reached for the cold black receiver of the telephone.

"Jon—" she said.

"It's my son." He picked up the receiver. "Jon Towers speaking."

"Call for you, Mr. Towers. Personal from Toronto from a Miss Sarah—"

"Just a minute." He thrust the receiver into the pillow, muffling it. "Go into the bathroom," he said to the woman. "It's a private call for me. Wait in the bathroom till I've finished."

"But—"

"Get out!"

She went without a word. The bathroom door closed softly behind her and he was alone.

"Thank you," he said into the receiver. "I'll take the call now."

The line clicked and hummed. A voice said, "I have Mr. Towers for you," and then Sarah's voice, very clear and gentle, said, "Jon?" rather doubtfully as if she found it hard to believe she could really be talking to him across the entire length of the Atlantic Ocean.

"Sarah," he said, and suddenly there were hot tears pricking his eyes and an ache in his throat. "I was going to phone you."

"Yes, I know," she said happily, "but I simply couldn't wait to tell you so I thought I'd ring first. Johnny, Aunt Mildred has come back to London a week early from her cruise—she got off at Tangier or something stupid because she didn't like the food—and so I've now got a fully qualified chaperone earlier than I expected! Is it all right if I fly over to London the day after tomorrow?"

61

Three

I

AFTER JON had replaced the receiver he sat motionless on the edge of the bed for a long moment. Presently the woman came out of the bathroom and paused by the door, leaning her back against the panels as she waited for him to look up and notice her.

"You'd better go," he said at last, not looking at her. "I'm sorry."

She hesitated, and then picked up her coat and slipped it quietly over her dress without replying straight away. But after a moment she said, "How long will you be in London?"

"I'm not sure."

She hesitated again, toying with the clasp of her handbag as if she could not make up her mind what to say. "Maybe I'll see you again if there's time," she said suddenly. "You've got my phone number, haven't you?"

He stood up then, looking her straight in the eyes, and she knew instinctively she had said the wrong thing. She felt her cheeks burn, a trick she thought she had outgrown years ago, and suddenly she was furious with him, furious at his casual invitation to his hotel, furious at the casual way he was dismissing her, furious because his casual manner was an enigma which she found as fascinating as it was infuriating.

"Have a lovely wedding, won't you," she said acidly in her softest, sweetest voice as she swept over to the door. "I hope your fiancée realizes the kind of man she's marrying."

She had the satisfaction of seeing the color drain from his face, and then the next moment she was gone, slamming the door behind her, and Jon was again alone with his thoughts in his room on the sixth floor.

II

After a long while it occurred to him to glance at his watch. It was late, well after midnight, and Justin should have phoned an hour ago. Jon sat still for a moment, his thoughts swiftly recalling the evening's events. Perhaps Camilla had forgotten to ask Justin to phone the hotel. Or maybe she hadn't forgotten but had deliberately withheld the message out of malice. Perhaps she also knew where Marijohn was and had lied when she had told him otherwise. . . . But no, Rivers had said he was the only one who had any form of contact with Marijohn, so Camilla had been telling the truth.

Michael Rivers.

Jon leaned over on the bed, propping himself up on one elbow, and picked up the telephone receiver.

"Yes, sir?" said a helpful voice a moment later.

"I want to call number five, Consett Mews, W.8. I don't know the number."

"Thank you, sir. If you would like to replace the receiver we'll ring you when we've put through your call."

The minutes passed noiselessly. The room was still and peaceful. After a while Jon idly began to tidy the bed, straightening the counterpane and smoothing the pillows in an attempt to smother his impatience by physical movement, and then the bell rang and he picked up the receiver again.

63

"Your number is ringing for you, Mr. Towers."

"Thank you."

The line purred steadily. No one answered. They're in bed, thought Jon, half-asleep and cursing the noise of the bell.

He waited, listening to the relentless ringing at the other end of the wire. Ten . . . Eleven . . . Twelve . . .

"Knightsbridge five-seven-eight-one."

This was an unknown voice. It was quiet, very distinct and even self-possessed.

"I want," said Jon, "to speak to Justin Towers."

"Speaking."

There was a silence. God Almighty, thought Jon suddenly. To his astonishment he noticed that his free hand was a clenched fist, and felt his heart hurting his lungs as he drew a deep breath to speak. And then the words wouldn't come and he could only sit and listen to the silence at the other end of the wire and the stillness in the room around him.

He tried to pull himself together. "Justin."

"Yes, I'm still here."

"Did your grandmother tell you I'd called at the Mews this evening?"

"Yes, she did."

"Then why didn't you phone when you arrived back? Didn't she tell you that I wanted you to phone me?"

"Yes, she did."

Silence. There was something very uncommunicative about the quiet voice and the lack of hesitation. Perhaps he was shy.

"Look, Justin, I want to see you very much—there's a lot I have to discuss with you. Can you come round to the hotel, as soon as possible tomorrow morning? What time can you manage?"

"I'm afraid I can't manage tomorrow," said the quiet voice. "I'm going out for the day."

Jon felt as though someone had just thrown an ice-cold towel in his face. He gripped the receiver tightly and sat forward a little further on the edge of the bed.

"Justin, do you know why I've come to Europe?"

"My grandmother said you were here to get married."

"I could have married in Toronto. I came to England especially to see you."

No reply. Perhaps the nightmare was a reality and he simply wasn't interested.

"I have a business proposition to make you," said Jon, fumbling for an approach which would appeal to this impersonal voice a mile away from him in Knightsbridge. "I'm very anxious to discuss it with you as soon as possible. Can't you put off your engagement tomorrow?"

"All right," said the voice indifferently after a pause. "I suppose so."

"Can you have breakfast with me?"

"I'm afraid I'm very bad at getting up on Saturday mornings."

"Lunch?"

"I'm—not sure."

"Well, come as soon after breakfast as you can and then we can talk for a while and maybe you can have lunch with me afterwards."

"All right."

"Fine," said Jon. "Don't forget to come, will you? I'll see you tomorrow."

After he had replaced the receiver he sat for ten seconds on the edge of the bed and stared at the silent telephone. Presently when he went into the bathroom, he saw that there was sweat on his forehead

65

and his hands as he raised them to flick the sweat away were trembling with tension. This is my mother's fault, he thought; she's turned the boy against me just as she tried to turn me against my father. When I meet Justin tomorrow he'll be a stranger and the fault will be hers.

He felt desolate suddenly, as if he had taken years of accumulated savings to the bank only to have them stolen from him as he approached the counter to hand over the money. He had a shower and undressed, but the desolation was with him even as he slid into bed, and he knew he would never be able to sleep. He switched out the light. It was after one o'clock, but the night yawned effortlessly ahead of him, hours of restless worry and anxiety, a steady deepening of the pain behind his eyes and the ache of tension in his body. The thoughts whirled and throbbed in his brain, sometimes mere patterns of consciousness, sometimes forming themselves into definite words and sentences.

Sarah would be coming to London in two days' time. Supposing Eve made trouble . . . He could pay her off for a time, but in the end something would have to be done. If only he could find Marijohn . . . but no one knew where she was, no one at all except Michael Rivers. Hell to Michael Rivers. How could one make a man like Michael talk? No good offering him money. No good urging or pleading or cajoling. Nothing was any good with a man like that. . . . But something would have to be done. Why did no one know where Marijohn was? The statement seemed to imply she was completely withdrawn from circulation. Perhaps she was abroad. Perhaps there was some man. She wouldn't live with Michael any more, Camilla had said; no doubt there were affairs too.

But that was all wrong. There would have been no real affairs. No real affairs.

But no one knew where Marijohn was and something would have to be done. Perhaps Justin would know. Justin . . .

The desolation nagged at him again, stabbing his consciousness with pain. Better not to think of Justin. And then without warning he was thinking of Clougy, aching for the soft breeze from the sea, pining for the white shutters and yellow walls and the warm mellow sense of peace. . . . Yet that was all gone, destroyed with Sophia's death. The sadness of it made him twist over in bed and bury his face deep in the pillow. He had forgotten until that moment how much he had loved his house in Cornwall.

He sat up in bed, throwing back the beclothes and going over to the window. "I want to talk about Clougy," he thought to himself, staring out into the night. "I want to talk about Sophia and why our marriage went so wrong when I loved her so much I could hardly bear to spend a single night away from her. I want to talk about Max and why our friendship was so completely destroyed that we were relieved to go our separate ways and walk out of each other's lives without a backward glance. I want to talk about Michael who never liked me because I conformed to no rules and was like no other man he had ever had to deal with in his narrow little legal world in London. I want to talk about Justin whom I loved because he was always cheerful and happy and comfortable in his plumpness, and because like me he enjoyed being alive and found all life exciting. And most of all I want to talk to Marijohn because I can discuss Clougy with no one except her. . . ."

He went back to bed, his longing sharp and jagged

in his mind, and tossed and turned restlessly for another hour. And then just before dawn there was suddenly a great inexplicable peace soothing his brain and he knew that at last he would be able to sleep.

III

After he had breakfasted the next morning, he went into the open lounge in the hotel lobby and sat down with a newspaper to wait for Justin to arrive. There was a constant stream of people crossing the lobby and entering or leaving the hotel, and at length he put the paper aside and concentrated on watching each person who walked through the swinging doors a few feet away from him.

Ten o'clock came. Then half-past. Perhaps he had changed his mind and decided not to come. If he wasn't going to come he should have phoned. But of course he would come. Why shouldn't he? He had agreed to it. He wouldn't back out now. . . .

A family of Americans arrived with a formidable collection of white suitcases. A young man who might easily have been Justin drifted in and then walked up to a girl who was sitting reading near Jon in the lounge. There was an affectionate reunion and they left together. A couple of foreign business men came in speaking a language that was either Danish or Swedish, and just behind them was another foreigner, dark and not very tall, who looked as though he came from Southern Europe. Italy, perhaps, or Spain. The two Scandinavian business men moved slowly over towards one of the other lounges, their heads bent in earnest conversation, their hands behind their backs like a couple of naval officers. The young Italian made no attempt to follow them. He walked slowly over to the reception desk instead, and asked for Mr. Jon Towers.

"I think, sir," said the uniformed attendant to him, that Mr. Towers is sitting in one of the armchairs behind you to your left."

The young man turned.

His dark eyes were serious and watchful, his features impassive. His face was plain but unusual. Jon recognized the small snub nose and the high cheekbones but not the gravity in the wide mouth nor the leanness about his jaw.

He walked across, very unhurried and calm. Jon stood up, knocking the ash-tray off the table and showering ashes all over the carpet.

"Hullo," said Justin, holding out his hand politely. "How are you?"

Jon took the hand in his, not knowing what to do with it, and then let it go. If only it had been ten years ago, he thought. There would have been no awkwardness, no constraint, no polite empty phrases and courteous gestures.

He smiled uncertainly at the young man beside him. "But you're so thin, Justin!" was all he could manage to say, "You're so slim and streamlined!"

The young man smiled faintly, gave a shrug of the shoulders which reminded Jon instantly and sickeningly of Sophia, and glanced down at the spilt ashes on the floor.

There was silence.

"Let's sit down," said Jon. "No point in standing. Do you smoke?"

"No, thank you."

They both sat down. Jon lit a cigarette.

"What are you doing now? Are you working?"

"Yes. Insurance in the city."

"Do you like it?"

"Yes."

"How did you get on at school? Where were you sent in the end?"

Justin told him.

"Did you like it?"

"Yes."

There seemed suddenly so little to say. Jon felt sick and ill and lost. "I expect you'd like me to come to the point," he said abruptly. "I came over here to ask you if you'd be interested in working in Canada with a view eventually to controlling a branch of my business based in London. I haven't opened this branch yet, but I intend to do so within the next three years. Ultimately, of course, if you made a success of the opportunity I would transfer the entire business to you when I retire. My business is property. It's a multi-million dollar concern."

He stopped. The lounge hummed with other people's steady conversation. People were still coming back and forth through the swing-doors into the hotel.

"I don't think," said Justin, "I should like to work in Canada."

A man and woman near them got up laughing. The woman had on a ridiculous yellow hat with a purple feather in it. The stupid things one noticed.

"Any particular reason?"

"Well . . ." Another vague shrug of the shoulders. "I'm quite happy in England. My grandmother's very good to me and I've got plenty of friends and so on. I like working in London and I've got a good opening in the City."

He was reddening slowly as he spoke, Jon noticed. His eyes were still watching the spilt ashes on the floor.

Jon said nothing.

"There's another reason too," said the boy, as if he sensed his other reasons hadn't been good enough. "There's a girl—someone I know. . . . I don't want to go away and leave her just yet."

"Marry her and come to Canada together."

Justin looked up startled, and Jon knew then that he had been lying. "But I can't—"

"Why not? I married when I was your age. You're old enough to know your own mind."

"It's not a question of marriage. We're not even engaged."

"Then she can't be so important to you that you would ignore a million-dollar opening in Canada to be with her. Okay, so you've got friends in England—you'd find plenty more in Canada. Okay, so your grandmother's been good to you—fine, but what if she has? You're not going to remain shackled to her all your life, are you? And what if you have got a good opening in the City? So have dozens of young men. I'm offering you the opportunity of a lifetime, something unique and dynamic and exciting. Don't you want to be your own master of your own business? Haven't you got the drive and ambition to want to take up a challenge and emerge the winner? What do you want of life? The nine-till-five stagnation of the city and years of comfortable boredom or the twenty-four hour excitement of juggling with millions of dollars? All right, so you're fond of London! I'm offering you the opportunity to come back here in three years' time, and when you come back you'll be twenty times richer than any of the friends you said good-bye to when you left for Canada. Hasn't the prospect any appeal to you at all? I felt so sure from all my memories of you that you wouldn't say no to an opportunity like this."

But the dark eyes were still expressionless, his face immobile. "I don't think property is really my line at all."

"Do you know anything about it?"

Justin was silent.

"Look, Justin—"

"I don't want to," said the boy rapidly. "I expect you could find someone else. I don't see why it has to be me."

"For Christ's sake!" Jon was almost beside himself with anger and despair. "What is it, Justin? What's happened? Don't you understand what I'm trying to say? I've been away from you for ten whole years and now I want to give you all I can to try and make amends. I want you to come into business with me so we'll never be separated again for long and so that I can get to know you and try to catch up on all the lost years. Don't you understand? Don't you see?"

"Yes," said Justin woodenly, "but I'm afraid I can't help you."

"Has your grandmother been talking to you? Has she? Has she been trying to turn you against me? What has she said?"

"She's never mentioned you."

"She must have!"

The boy shook his head and glanced down at his watch. "I'm afraid—"

"No," said Jon. "No, you're not going yet. Not till I've got to the bottom of all this."

"I'm sorry, but—"

"Sit down." He grasped the boy's arm and pulled him back into his chair. Justin wrenched himself away. "There's one question I'm going to ask you whether you like it or not, and you're not leaving till you've given me a proper answer."

He paused. The boy made no move but merely stared sullenly into his eyes.

"Justin, why did you never answer my letters?"

The boy still stared but his eyes were different. The sullenness had been replaced by a flash of bewilderment and suspicion which Jon did not understand.

"Letters?"

"You remember when I said good-bye to you after I took you away from Clougy?"

The suspicion was gone. Only the bewilderment remained. "Yes."

"You remember how I explained that I couldn't take you with me, as I would have no home and no one to help look after you, and you had to go to an English school? You remember how I promised to write, and how I made you promise you would answer my letters and tell me all you'd been doing?"

The boy didn't speak this time. He merely nodded.

"Then why didn't you write? You promised you would. I wrote you six letters including a birthday present, but I never had a word from you. Why was it, Justin? Was it because you resented me not taking you to Canada? I only did it for your own good. I would have come back to see you, but I got caught up in my business interests, so involved that it was hard even to get away for the odd weekend. But I wanted to see you and hear from you all the time, yet nothing ever came. In the end I stopped writing because I thought that in some strange way the letters must be hurting you, and at Christmas and on your birthday I merely sent over money to be paid into your trust fund at your grandmother's bank. . . . What happened, Justin? Was it something to do with that last time at Clougy when—"

"I have to go," said the boy, and he was stammering,

his composure shattered. "I—I'm sorry, but I must go. Please." He was standing up, stumbling towards the swinging doors, not seeing nor caring where he went.

The doors opened and swung in a flash of bright metal, and then Jon was alone once more in his hotel and the failure was a throbbing, aching pain across his heart.

IV

It was eleven o'clock when Justin arrived back at Consett Mews. His grandmother, who was writing letters in the drawing room, looked up, startled by his abrupt entrance.

"Justin—" He saw her expression change almost imperceptibly as she saw his face. "Darling, what's happened? What did he say? Did he—"

He stood still, looking at her. She stopped.

"What happened," he said, "to the letters my father sent me from Canada ten years ago?"

He saw her blush, an ugly red stain beneath the careful make-up, and in a sudden sickening moment he thought, Its true. He did write. She lied to me all the time.

"Letters?" she said. "From Canada?"

"He wrote me six letters. And sent a birthday present."

"Is that what he said?" But it was only a halfhearted attempt at defense. She took a step towards him, making an impulsive gesture with her hands. "I only did it for your own good, darling. I thought it would only upset you to read letters from him when he had left you behind and gone to Canada without you."

"Did you read the letters?"

74

"No," she said at once. "No, I—"

"You let six letters come to me from my father and you destroyed them to make me think he had forgotten me entirely?"

"Justin, no, Justin, you don't understand—"

"You never had any letters from him so you didn't want me to have letters from him either!"

"No," she said, "no, it wasn't like that—"

"You lied and deceived and cheated me year after year, day after day—"

"It was for your own good, Justin, your own good . . ."

She sat down again as if he had exhausted all her strength, and suddenly she was old to him, a woman with a lined, tear-stained face and bent shoulders and trembling hands. "Your father cares nothing for anyone except himself," he heard her whisper at last. "He takes people and uses them for his own ends, so that although you care for him your love is wasted because he never cares for you. I've been useful to him at various times, providing him with a home when he was young, looking after you when he was older—but he's never cared. You'll be useful to him now to help him with his business in Canada. Oh, don't think I can't guess why he wanted to see you! But he'll never care for you yourself, only for your usefulness to him—"

"You're wrong," said Justin. "He does care. You don't understand."

"Understand! I understand all too well!"

"I don't believe you understood him any better than you understood me."

"Justin—"

"I'm going to Canada with him."

There was a moment of utter silence.

"You can't," she said at last. "Please, Justin. Be sensible. You're talking of altering your whole career, damaging all your prospects in London, just because of a ten-minute meeting this morning with a man you hardly know. Please, please be sensible and don't talk like this."

"I've made up my mind."

Camilla looked at him, the years blurring before her eyes, and suddenly the boy before her was Jon saying in that same level, obstinate voice which she had come to dread so much: "I've made up my mind. I'm going to marry her."

"You're a fool, Justin," she said, her voice suddenly harsh and clear. "You've no idea what you're doing. You know nothing about your father at all."

He turned aside and moved towards the door. "I'm not listening to this."

"Of course," said Camilla, "You're too young to remember what happened at Clougy."

"Shut up!" he shouted, whirling to face her. "Shut up, shut up!"

"I wasn't there, but I can guess what happened. He drove your mother to death, you do realize that, don't you? The jury said the death was accidental, but I always knew it was suicide. The marriage was finished, and once that was gone there was nothing else left for her. Of course anyone could have foreseen the marriage wouldn't last! Her attraction for him was entirely sexual and after several years of marriage it was only natural that he should become bored with her. It was the same old story—she cared for him, but basically he never cared for her, only for the pleasure she could give him in bed. And once the pleasure had been replaced by boredom she meant nothing to him at all. So he started to look round for some other woman. It had to be some woman who was quite different, preferably someone rather aloof and unobtainable, because that made the task of conquest so much more interesting and exciting. And during the weekend that your mother died, just such a woman happened to be staying at Clougy. Of course you never knew that he and Marijohn—"

Justin's hands were over his ears, shutting her voice from his mind as he stumbled into the hall and banged the door shut behind him. Then, after running up the stairs two at a time, he reached his room, found a suitcase and started to pack his belongings.

V

It was noon. On the sixth floor of the Mayfair Hotel, Jon was sitting in his room working out an advertisement for the personal column of the *Times* and wondering whether there would be any point in trying to see Michael Rivers again. Before him on the table lay his penciled note of Eve's telephone number, and as he worried over the problem he picked up the slip of paper idly and bent it between his fingers. He would have to get in touch with the woman to get to the bottom of this business of the anonymous phone call, but if only he could find Marijohn first it would be easier to know which line to adopt. . . . He was just tossing the scrap of paper aside and concentrating on his message for the *Times* when the phone rang.

He picked up the receiver. "Yes?"

"There's a lady here to see you, Mr. Towers."

"Does she give her name?"

"No, sir."

It would be Eve ready to lay her cards on the table. "All right, I'll come down."

He replaced the receiver, checked the money in his

wallet and went out. Canned music was still playing in the lift. On the ground floor he walked out into the lobby and crossed over to the leather chairs of the open lounge below the reception desk.

His mind saw her the instant before his eyes did. He had a moment of searing relief mingled with a burst of blazing joy, and then he was moving forward again towards her and Marijohn was smiling into his eyes.

II

One

I

SARAH SPENT the journey across the Atlantic alternating between a volume of John Clare's poetry and the latest mystery by a well-known crime writer. Occasionally it occurred to her that she hadn't understood a word she was reading and that it would be much more sensible to put both books away, but still she kept them on her lap and watched the written page from time to time. And then at last, the lights of London lay beneath the plane, stretching as far as the eye could see, and she felt the old familiar feeling of nervousness tighten beneath her heart as she thought of Jon.

She loved Jon and knew perfectly well that she wanted to marry him, but he remained an enigma to her at times and it was this strange unknown quality which made her nervous. She called it the Distant Mood. She could understand Jon when he was gay, excited, nervous, musical, sad, disappointed or merely obstinate, but Jon in the Distant Mood was something which frightened her because she knew neither the cause of the mood nor the correct response to it. Her nervousness usually reduced her to silence, and her silence led to a sense of failure, hard to explain. Perhaps, she had thought, it would be different in England; he would be far from the worries and troubles of his work, and perhaps when he was in an easier, less complex frame of mind she would be able to say to him: "Jon, why is it that sometimes you're so far away that I don't know how to reach out to communicate with you? Why is it that sometimes you're so abrupt I feel I mustn't talk for fear of making you lose your temper and quarrel? Is the fault mine? Is it that I don't understand something in you or that I do something to displease you? If it's my fault, tell me what I'm doing wrong so that I can put it right, because I can't bear it when you're so far away and remote and indifferent to the world."

He had been in the Distant Mood when she had telephoned him in London two nights ago. She had recognized it at once, and although she had done her best to sound gay and cheerful, she had cried when she had replaced the receiver. That had led to the inevitable scene with her parents.

"Sarah dear, if there's any doubt in your mind, don't . . ."

"Far better to be sorry now than be sorry after you're married."

"I mean, darling, I know you're very lucky to be marrying Jon. In many ways your father and I both like him very much, but all the same, he's many years older than you and of course, it *is* difficult when you marry out of your generation. . . ."

And Sarah had very stupidly lost her temper in the face of these platitudes and had locked herself in her room to face a sleepless night on her own.

The next day had been spent in packing and preparing for the journey to London on the following day. He would phone that night, she had thought. He would be certain to phone that night, and when he talked he would sound quite different and everything would be all right again.

But the phone call never came.

Her mother had decided Sarah's distress was due to

pre-marital nerves and had talked embarrassingly for five whole minutes littered with awkward pauses on the intimate side of marriage. In the end, Sarah had gone out to the nearest cinema to escape and had seen an incredibly bad epic film on a wide screen which had given her a headache. It had been almost a relief to board the plane for London the following day and take a definite course of action at last after so much restless waiting and anxiety.

The plane drifted lower and lower over the mass of lights until Sarah could see the landing lights of the runway rising from the ground to meet them, and then there were the soft thumps of landing and the long cruise to a halt on English soil. Outside the plane, the air was damp and cool. The trek through customs came next, her nerves tightening steadily as the minutes passed, until at last she was moving into the great central lobby and straining her eyes for a glimpse of Jon.

Something had gone wrong. He wasn't there. He was going to break off the engagement. He had had an accident, was injured, dying, dead. . . .

"God Almighty," said Jon's voice just behind her. "I thought you were a white sheet at first! Who's been frightening the life out of you?"

The relief was a great cascading warmth making her limbs relax and the tears spring to her eyes.

"Oh Jon, Jon."

There was no Distant Mood this time. He was smiling, his eyes brilliantly alive, his arms very strong, and when he kissed her it seemed ridiculous that she should ever have had any worries at all.

"You look," he said, "quite frighteningly sophisticated. What's all this green eye-shadow and mud on your eyelashes?"

"Oh Jon, I spent hours—" She laughed suddenly in

a surge of happiness and he laughed too, kissing her again and then sliding his arm round her waist.

"Am I covered in Canada's most soigné lipstick?"

He was. She produced a handkerchief and carefully wiped it off.

"Right," he said briskly, when she had finished. "Let's go. There's dinner waiting for us at the Hilton and endless things to be discussed before I take you to your Aunt Mildred's, so we've no time to waste. . . . Is this all your luggage or has Cleopatra got another gold barge full of suitcases sailing up the customs' conveyor belt?"

There was a taxi waiting and then came the journey into the heart of London, through the Middlesex suburbs to Kensington, Knightsbridge and the Park. The warmth of London hummed around them, the roar of engines revved in their ears, and Sarah, her hand clasped tightly in Jon's, thought how exciting it was to come home at last to her favorite city and to travel through the brightly-lit streets to the resplendent glamour of a lush, expensive world.

"How's Cleopatra feeling now?"

"Thinking how much nicer than Mark Antony you are and how much better than Alexandria London is."

He laughed. She was happy. When they reached the Hilton she had a moment's thrill as she crossed the threshold into the luxury which was still new to her, and then they were in the diningroom and she was trying hard to pretend she was quite accustomed to dining in the world's most famous restaurants.

Jon ordered the meal, chose the wines and tossed both menu and wine-list on one side.

"Sarah, there are a lot of things I have to discuss with you."

84

Of course, she thought. The wedding and honeymoon. Exciting, breath-taking plans.

"First of all, I want to apologize for not phoning you last night. I became very involved with my family and there were various difficulties. I hope you'll forgive me and understand."

She smiled thankfully, eager to forgive. "Of course, Jonny. I thought something like that must have happened."

"Secondly I have to apologize for my manner on the phone the other night. I'm afraid I must have sounded very odd indeed but again I was heavily involved with other things and I wasn't expecting you to call. I hope you didn't think I wasn't pleased that you were going to come over to England earlier than expected. It was a wonderful surprise."

"You—did sound a little strange."

"I know." He picked up the wine-list and put it down again restlessly. "Let me try and explain what's been happening. I arrived here to find my mother had left her house in Halkin Street, so naturally I had to spend time tracing her before I could go and see her. That all took time, and then I managed to meet Justin and have a talk with him—"

"You did?" She had heard all about Justin, and Jon's plans to invite him to Canada. "Is it all right? What did he say?"

"He's coming to Canada. He hesitated at first, but now he's made up his mind, so that's all settled, thank God." He unfolded the table napkin absentmindedly and fingered the soft linen. "Then there were various other people I had to see—Max Alexander, an old friend of mine, for instance . . . and various others. I haven't had much time to spare since I arrived."

"No, you must have been very busy." She watched

his restless fingers. "What about the wedding, Jonny, and the honeymoon? Or haven't you had much chance to make any more definite arrangements yet?"

"That," said Jon, "is what I want to talk to you about."

The first course arrived with the first wine. Waiters flitted around the table and then withdrew in a whirl of white coats.

"What do you mean, darling?"

He took a mouthful of hors d'oeuvre and she had to wait a moment for his reply. Then: "I want to get married right away," he said suddenly, looking straight into her eyes. "I can get a special license and we can be married just as soon as possible. Then maybe a honeymoon in Spain, Italy, Paris—wherever you like, and a few days in England before we fly back to Canada with Justin."

She stared at him, the thoughts whirling dizzily in her brain. "But Jon, Mummy and Daddy aren't here. I—I haven't bought all the trousseau. . . . I was waiting till Mummy was here before I bought the last few things—"

"Hell to the trousseau. I don't care if you come away with me dressed in a sack. And why can't you go shopping without your mother? I'm sure your taste is just as good if not better than hers."

"But Jon—"

"Do you really feel you can't get married without your parents being here?"

She swallowed, feeling as if she was on a tightrope struggling to keep her balance. "I—I just want to be fair to them, and—and I know . . . Yes, I do want them to be here, Jon, I really do. . . . But if—I just don't understand. Why are you in such a hurry to get married all of a sudden?"

He looked at her. She felt herself blush without knowing why, and suddenly she was afraid, afraid of the Distant Mood, afraid of hurting her parents, afraid of the wedding and the first night of the honeymoon.

"Jon, I—"

"I'm sorry," he said, his hand closing on hers across the table. "That was wrong of me. Of course you shall have your parents here. I was just being selfish and impatient."

"Perhaps I'm the one who's being selfish," she said ashamed. "I did say I wanted a quiet wedding—"

"But not as quiet as the one I've just suggested." He wasn't angry. "It's all right—I understand. We'll keep it the way you want it. After all, the actual wedding will be much more important to you than to me. That's only natural."

"I suppose so," she said, struggling to understand. "The wedding's the bride's day, isn't it? And then, of course, you've been married before so—"

"So I'm blasé about it!" he teased, and she smiled.

They concentrated on the hors d'oeuvre for a few minutes.

"Sarah."

Something else was coming. She could sense her nerves tightening and her heart thudding a shade quicker as she waited.

"No matter when we get married, I would like to talk to you a little about Sophia."

She took a sip of wine steadily, trying to ignore the growing tension in her limbs. "You needn't talk about her if you don't want to, Jon. I understand."

"I don't want you to get one of these dreadful first-wife complexes," he said, laying down his knife and fork and slumping back in his chair. "Don't for God's sake, start imagining Sophia to be something so exotic that you can hardly bear to tip-toe in her footsteps. She

87

was a very ordinary girl with a lot of sex-appeal. I married her because I was young enough to confuse lust with love. It's quite a common mistake, I believe." He drained his glass and toyed idly with the stem as his eyes glanced round the room. "For awhile we were very happy, and then she became bored and I found I could no longer love her or confide in her as I had when I married her. We quarreled a lot. And then, just as I was thinking of the idea of divorce, she had the accident and died. It was complete and utter hell for me and for everyone else who was staying at Clougy at the time, especially as the inquest had a lot of publicity in the local papers and all sorts of rumors started to circulate. One rumor even said that I'd killed her. No doubt some vicious-minded crank had heard we weren't on the best of terms and had drawn his own melodramatic conclusions when he heard that Sophia had fallen down the cliff path and broken her neck on the rocks below. . . . But it was an accident. The jury said it could have been suicide because she wasn't happy at Clougy, but that was ridiculous. They didn't know Sophia and how much she loved life—even if life merely consisted of living at Clougy far from the glamor of London. Her death was an accident. There's no other explanation."

She nodded. Waiters came and went. Another course was laid before her.

"And anyway," said Jon, "why would I have wanted to kill her? Divorce is the civilized method of discarding an unwanted spouse, and I had no reason to prefer murder to divorce." He started to eat. "However, I'm wandering from the point. I just wanted to tell you that you needn't ever worry that you're inadequate compared to Sophia, because there simply is no comparison. I love you in many different ways and Sophia I only

88

loved in one way—and even that way turned sour in the end. . . . You understand, don't you? You follow what I'm saying?"

"Yes, Jon," she said. "I understand." But her thoughts, the most private of her thoughts which she would never have disclosed to anyone, whispered: She must have been very good in bed. Supposing . . . And then, even her private thoughts subsided into a mass of blurred fears and worries which she automatically pushed to the furthest reaches of her mind.

Jon was smiling at her across the table, the special message of laughter and love in his eyes. "You still want to marry me?"

She smiled back, and suddenly she loved him so much that nothing mattered in all the world except her desire to be with him and make him happy. "Yes," she said impulsively. "I do. But don't let's wait for my parents, Jonny—I've changed my mind. Let's get married right away after all. . . ."

II

At half-past eleven that night, Jon dialed a London telephone number.

"Everything's fine," he said into the receiver presently. "We're marrying this week, honeymoon in Paris for ten days, a pause for a day or two in London to collect Justin, and then we all go back to Canada—and well away from the anonymous phone caller and any danger of Sarah finding out anything. It's best for her not to know."

A pause.

"Yes, I did. No trouble at all. She didn't even ask

any questions about Sophia. I concentrated on the angle you suggested."

Another pause. The night deepened. Then: "How will I explain to her? It'll look pretty damned odd if I go back there, especially in view of my conversation with her tonight about Sophia. . . . Why yes, of course! Yes, that's reasonable enough . . . All right, I'll see you in about a fortnight's time, then. Good-bye, darling . . . and think of me."

III

The hotel in Paris was very large and grand and comfortable, and Sarah beneath her gay smile and excited eyes felt very small and lost and nervous. Later in the evening at the famous restaurant she tried to do justice to the food that was placed before her, but the nervousness and tension only increased until she could not eat any more. And then at last they returned to the hotel, said goodnight to the team on duty at the reception desk and travelled up in the elevator to their suite on the first floor.

Jon wandered into the bathroom. As Sarah undressed slowly she heard the hiss of the shower, and knew that she would have a few minutes to herself. She tried not to think of Sophia. What would Sophia have done on her wedding night? She wouldn't have sat trembling through an exotic dinner or spent precious minutes fumbling to undress herself with leaden fingers. . . . Perhaps Jon had lived with Sophia before he had married her. He had never asked Sarah to do such a thing, but then of course she was different, and Sophia had been so very attractive—and foreign. . . . Being foreign probably made a difference. Or did it?

She sat down at the dressing-table in her nightdress and fidgeted uncertainly with her hair. I wonder what Sophia looked like, she thought. I've never asked Jon. But she must have been dark like Justin, and probably slim and supple. Darker and slimmer than I am, I expect. And more attractive, of course. Oh God, how angry Jon would be if he could hear me! I must stop thinking of Sophia.

Jon came back from the bathroom and threw his clothes carelessly into an armchair. He was naked.

"Perhaps I'll have a bath," said Sarah to her fingernails. "Would it matter, do you think?"

"Not in the least," said Jon, "except that we'll both be rather hot in bed."

The bathroom was a reassuring prison of steam and warmth. The bath took a long time to run, almost as long as it took her to wash. She lingered, drying herself and then paused to sit on the stool as the tears started to prick her eyes. She tried to fight them back, and then suddenly she was caught in a violent wave of homesickness and the tears refused to be checked. The room swam, the sobs twisted and hurt her throat as she fought against them, and she was just wondering how she would ever have the strength to return to the bedroom when Jon tried the handle of the locked door.

"Sarah?"

She wept soundlessly, not answering.

"Can you let me in?"

She tried to speak but could not.

"Please."

Dashing away her tears she stumbled to the door and unlocked it. As she returned blindly to the stool and the mirror she heard Jon come in. She waited, dreading his mood, praying he wouldn't be too angry.

"Sarah," she heard him say. "Darling Sarah." And suddenly he had taken her gently in his arms as if she had been very small, and was pressing her tightly to him in a clumsy comforting gesture which she found unexpectedly moving. She had never before thought him capable of great tenderness. "You're thinking of Sophia," he whispered in her ear. "I wish you wouldn't. Please, Sarah, don't think of Sophia any more."

The fears ebbed from her mind; when he stooped his head to kiss her on the mouth at last she was conscious first and foremost of the peace in her heart before her world quickened and whirled into the fire.

IV

When they arrived back in London ten days later, Jon spent two hours making involved transatlantic telephone calls and dealing with various urgent business commitments; his right-hand man, whom Sarah had met in Canada, had flown to Europe for some reason connected with the business, and the first night in town was spent in dining with him at a well-known restaurant. On the following day they had lunch with Camilla in Knightsbridge. When they were travelling back to their hotel afterwards, Sarah turned to Jon with a puzzled expression in her eyes.

"Where was Justin? He was never mentioned, so I didn't like to ask."

"There was a slight awkwardness when he decided he was going to Canada to work for me. After he had given in his notice and finished his work in the City I gave him some money and told him to go on holiday until I was ready to go back to Canada, and in fact he's gone down to Cornwall to stay with a cousin of mine."

"Oh, I see."

The taxi cruised gently out of the Hyde Park underpass and accelerated into Piccadilly. On the right lay the green trees of the park and the warmth of the summer sun on the short grass. It was hot.

"As a matter of fact," said Jon idly, glancing out of the window, "I'd rather like you to meet this cousin of mine. I thought maybe we might hire a car and drive down to Cornwall this weekend and spend a few days in the country before flying straight back to Canada."

Sarah glanced up at the cloudless sky and thought longingly of golden sands and waves breaking and curling towards the shore. "That sounds lovely, Jonny. I'd like to stay just a little longer in England, especially as the weather's so good now."

"You'd like to go?"

"Very much. Whereabouts does your cousin live?"

"Well . . ." He paused. The taxi approached the Ritz and had to wait at the traffic lights. "As it happens," he said at last, "she's now living at Clougy."

The lights flashed red and amber; a dozen engines throbbed in anticipation.

"When I left ten years ago," Jon said, "I never wanted to see the place again. I nearly sold it so that I could wash my hands of it once and for all, but at the last minute I changed my mind and gave it to my cousin instead. It was such a beautiful place, and so unique. I loved it better than any other place in the world at one time, and I suppose even after everything that had happened I was still too fond of the house to sell it to a stranger. My cousin goes back there once or twice a year and lets it for periods during the summer. I saw her briefly in London before you arrived, and when she talked of Clougy and how peaceful it was I found I had a sudden longing to go back just to see if I could ever find it peaceful again. I think perhaps I could now after ten years. I know I could never live there permanently again, but when my cousin suggested we go down to stay with her for a few days I felt so tempted to go back for a visit. . . . Can you understand? Or perhaps you would rather not go."

"No," she said automatically, "I don't mind at all. It won't have any memories for me. If you're willing to go back, Jon, then that's all that matters." But simultaneously she thought: How could he even think of going back? And her mind was confused and bewildered as she struggled to understand.

"It's mainly because of my cousin," he said, as if sensing her difficulties. "I'd love to have the chance to see her again and I know she's anxious to meet you."

"You've never mentioned her to me before," was all she could say. "Or is she one of the cousins on your mother's side of the family, the ones you said you wouldn't trouble to invite to the wedding?"

"No, Marijohn is my only relation on my father's side of the family. We spent a lot of time together until I was seven, and then after my parents' divorce my father took her away from the house where I lived with my mother and sent her to a convent. He was her guardian. I didn't see much of her after that until I was about fifteen, and my father returned to England for good to live in London and remove Marjohn from the convent. I saw a great deal of her then until I married and went down to Cornwall to live. I was very fond of her."

"Why didn't you invite her to the wedding?"

"I did mention it to her, but she couldn't come."

"Oh."

94

"I don't know why I didn't mention her to you before," he said vaguely as the taxi drew up outside the hotel. "I lost touch with her when I went to Canada and I didn't honestly expect to see her again when I returned. However, she heard I was in London and we had a brief meeting. . . . So much happened in those two days before you arrived, and then, of course, when you did arrive I forgot everything except the plans for the wedding and the honeymoon. But when I woke this morning and saw the sunshine and the blue sky I remembered her invitation to Clougy and started wondering about a visit to Cornwall. . . . You're sure you'd like to come? If you'd rather stay in London don't be afraid to say so."

"No, Jon," she said. "I'd like to spend a few days by the sea." And as she spoke she thought: There's still so much about Jon that I don't understand and yet he understands me through and through. Or does he? Perhaps if he really understood me he'd know I don't want to go to the house where he lived with his first wife. . . . But maybe I'm being unnecessarily sensitive. If he had an ancestral home I would go back there to live with him no matter how many times he'd been previously married, and wouldn't think it in the least strange. And Jon has no intention of living at Clougy again anyway; he's merely suggesting a short visit to see his cousin. I'm being absurd, working up a Sophia complex again. I must pull myself together.

"Tell me more about your cousin, Jon," she said as they got out of the taxi. "What did you say her name was?"

But when they went into the hall Jon's Canadian business associate crossed the lobby to meet them, and Marijohn wasn't mentioned again till later in the afternoon when Jon went up to their room to make two telephone calls, one to his cousin in Cornwall and the other to inquire about hiring a car to take them to St. Just. When he came back he was smiling and her uneasiness faded as she saw he was happy.

"We can have a car tomorrow," he said. "If we leave early we can easily do the journey in a day. We'll be a long way ahead of the weekend holiday traffic, and the roads shouldn't be too bad."

"And your cousin? Is she pleased?"

"Yes," said Jon, pushing back his hair in a luxurious, joyous gesture of comfort. "Very pleased indeed."

V

The sun was a burst of red above the sea by the time they reached the airport at St. Just, and as Jon swung the car off on to the road that led to Clougy, his frame seemed to vibrate with some fierce excitement which Sarah sensed but could not share. She glanced back over her shoulder at the soothing security of the little airport with its small plane waiting motionless on the runway, and then stared at the arid, sterile beauty of the Cornish moors.

"Isn't it wonderful?" said Jon to her, his hands gripping the wheel, his eyes blazing with joy. "Isn't it beautiful?"

And suddenly she was infected by his excitement so that the landscape no longer seemed repellant in its bleakness but fascinating in its austerity.

The car began to purr downhill; after a moment Sarah could no longer see the small huddle of the airport buildings with their hint of contact with the civilized world far away, and soon the car was travelling into a green valley dotted with isolated farms and squares of pasture bordered by gray stone walls. The road was single-track only now; the gradient was becoming steeper, and the sea was temporarily hidden from them by sloping hills. Soon they were passing the gates of a farm, and the next moment the car was grating from the smooth tarmac on to the rough uneven stones of a cart-track. As they passed the wall by the farm gate, Sarah was just able to catch a glimpse of a notice with an arrow pointing down the track, and above the arrow someone had painted the words "To Clougy."

The car crawled on, trickling downhill stealthily over the rough track. On either side the long grass waved gracefully in the soft breeze from the sea, and above them the sky was blue and cloudless.

"There's the water wheel," said Jon, and his voice was scarcely louder than an unspoken thought, his hands tightening again on the wheel in his excitement. "And there's Clougy."

The car drifted on to smoother ground and then turned into a small driveway. As the engine died Sarah heard for the first time the rushing water of the stream as it passed the disused water wheel on the other side of the track and tumbled down towards the sea.

"How quiet it is," she said automatically. "How peaceful after London."

Jon was already out of the car and walking toward the house. Opening her own door she stepped on to the gravel of the drive and stood still for a moment, glancing around her. There was a green lawn, not very big, with a white swing-seat at one end. The small garden was surrounded by clumps of rhododendron and other shrubs and there were trees, bent backwards into strange contorted shapes by the prevailing wind from the sea. She was standing at one side of the house but slightly in front of it so that from her angle she

97

could glimpse the yellow walls and white shutters as they basked in the summer sun. A bird sang, a cricket chirped and then there was silence, except for the rushing stream and, far away, the distant murmur of the tide on the pebbled beach.

"Sarah!" called Jon.

"Coming!" She stepped forward, still feeling mesmerized by the sense of peace, and as she moved she saw that he was in the shade of the porch waiting for her.

She drew closer, feeling absurdly vulnerable as she crossed the sunlit drive while he watched her from the shadows, and then she saw that he was not alone and the odd feeling of defenselessness increased. It must be a form of self-consciousness, she thought. She felt exactly as if she were some show exhibit being scrutinized and examined by a row of very critical judges. Ridiculous.

And then she saw the woman. There was a dull gleam of golden hair, the wide slant of remote eyes, the slight curve of a beautiful mouth, and as Sarah paused uncertainly, waiting for Jon to make the introductions, she became aware of an extreme stillness as if the landscape around them was tensed and waiting for something beyond her understanding.

Jon smiled at the woman. He made no effort to speak, but for some odd reason his silence didn't matter, and it suddenly occurred to Sarah that she had not heard one word exchanged between the two of them even though she had been well within earshot when they had met. She was just wondering if Jon had kissed his cousin, and was on the point of thinking that it was most unlikely that they would have embraced without some form of greeting, when the woman stepped from the shadows into the sunlight.

"Hullo, Sarah," she said. "I'm so glad you could come. Welcome to Clougy, my dear, and I hope you'll be very happy here."

Two

I

THEIR BEDROOM was filled with the afternoon sun, and as Sarah crossed to the window she saw the sea shimmering before her in the cove, framed by the twin hillsides on either side of the house. She caught her breath, just as she always did when she saw something very beautiful, and suddenly she was glad they had come and ashamed of all her misgivings.

"Have you got everything you want here?" said Marijohn, glancing round the room with the eye of a careful hostess. "Let me know if I've forgotten anything. Dinner will be in about half an hour, and the water's hot if you should want a bath."

"Thank you," said Sarah, turning to face her with a smile. "Thank you very much."

Jon was walking along the corridor just as Marijohn left the room. Sarah heard his footsteps pause.

"When's dinner? In about half an hour?"

Marijohn must have made some gesture of assent which she didn't say aloud. "I'll be in the kitchen for a while."

"We'll come down when we're ready, and have a drink." He walked into the room, closed the door behind him and yawned luxuriously, stretching every muscle with slow precision. "Well?" he inquired presently.

"Well?" She smiled at him.

"Do you like it?"

"Yes," she said. "It's very beautiful, Jon."

He kicked off his shoes, pulled off his shirt and waded out of his trousers. Before she turned back uneasily towards the window to watch the sun sparkling on the sea she saw him pull back the covers from the bed and then fling himself down on the smooth white linen.

"What shall I wear for dinner?" she said hesitantly. "Will Marijohn change?"

He didn't reply.

"Jon?"

"Yes?"

She repeated the question.

"I don't know," he said. "Does it matter?" His fingers were smoothing the linen restlessly, and his eyes were watching his fingers.

She said nothing, every nerve in her body slowly tightening as the silence became prolonged. She had almost forgotten how frightened she was of his Distant Mood.

"Come here a moment," he said abruptly, and then, as she gave a nervous start of surprise: "Good God, you nearly jumped out of your skin! What's the matter with you?"

"Nothing, Jon," she said, moving towards him. "Nothing at all."

He pulled her down on to the sheets beside him and kissed her several times on the mouth, throat and breasts. His hands started to hurt her. She was just wondering how she could escape from making love while he was in his present mood, when he rolled away from her and stood up lazily in one long fluent movement of his body. He still didn't speak. She watched him open a suitcase, empty the entire contents on to the floor and then survey the muddle without interest.

"What are you looking for, darling?"

He shrugged. Presently he found a shirt and there was a silence while he put it on. Then: "You must be tired after the journey," he said at last.

"A little." She felt ashamed, inadequate, tongue-tied.

For a moment she thought he wasn't going to say anything else but she was mistaken.

"Sex still doesn't interest you much, does it?"

"Yes, it does," she said in a low voice, the unwanted tears pricking at the back of her eyes. "It's just that it's still rather new to me and I'm not much good when you're rough and start to hurt."

He didn't answer. She saw him step into another pair of trousers and then, as he moved over to the basin to wash, everything became blurred and she could no longer see. Presently she found a dress amongst the luggage and started to change from her blouse and skirt, her movements automatic, her fingers stiff and clumsy as she fumbled with zip fastners and buttonholes.

"Are you ready?" he said at last.

"Yes, almost." She didn't dare stop to re-apply her lipstick. There was just time to brush her hair lightly into position and then they were going out into the corridor and moving downstairs to the drawing-room, the silence a thick invisible wall between them.

Marijohn was already there but Justin had apparently disappeared to his room. Sarah sat down, her limbs aching with tension, the lump of misery still, hurting her throat.

"What would you like to drink, Sarah?" said Marijohn.

"I—I don't mind. . . . Sherry or—or a martini—"

"I've some dry sherry. Would that do? What about you, Jon?"

Jon shrugged his shoulders again, not bothering to reply. Oh God, thought Sarah, how will she cope? Should I try to cover up for him? Oh Jon, Jon . . .

But Marijohn was pouring out a whisky and soda without waiting for him to answer. "I've enjoyed having Justin here," she said tranquilly, handing him his glass. "It's been fascinating getting to know him again. You remember how we used to puzzle over him, trying to decide who he resembled? It seems so strange now that there could ever have been any doubt."

Jon turned suddenly to face her. "Why?"

"He's like you, Jon. There's such a strong resemblance. It's quite uncanny sometimes."

"He doesn't look like me."

"What on Earth have looks got to do with it? Sarah, have a cocktail biscuit. Justin went specially to Penzance to buy some, so I suppose we'd better try and eat a few of them. . . . Jon darling, do sit down and stop being so restless—you make me feel quite exhausted, just sitting watching you. . . . That's better. Isn't the light unusual this evening? I have a feeling Justin has sneaked off somewhere to paint one of his secret water colors. . . . You must persuade him to show you some of them, Jon, because they're very good—or at least, they seem good to me, but then I know nothing about painting. . . . You paint, don't you, Sarah?"

"Yes," said Jon, before Sarah could reply, and suddenly his hand was on hers again and she knew in a hot rush of relief that the mood had passed. "She also happens to be an authority on the Impressionists and the Renaissance painters and the—"

"Jon, don't exaggerate!"

And the golden light of the evening seemed to deepen as they laughed and relaxed.

After dinner Jon took Sarah down to the cove to watch the sunset. The cove was small and rocky, its beach strewn with huge boulders and smooth pebbles, and as Jon found a suitable vantage point Sarah saw the fins of the Atlantic sharks coasting off-shore and moving slowly towards Cape Cornwall.

"I'm sorry," said Jon suddenly from beside her.

She nodded, trying to tell him without words that she understood, and then they sat down together and he put his arm round her shoulders, drawing her closer to him.

"What do you think of Marijohn?"

She thought for a moment, her eyes watching the light change on the sea, her ears full of the roar of the surf and the cry of the gulls. "She's very—" the words eluded her. Then: "—unusual," she said lamely at last, for lack of anything better to say.

"Yes," he said. "She is." He sounded tranquil and happy, and they sat for a while in silence as the sun began to sink into the sea.

"Jon."

"Yes?"

"Where—" She hesitated and then plunged on, reassured by his complete change of mood. "Where did Sophia—"

"Not here," he said at once. "It was farther along the cliff going south to Sennen. The cliff is shallow and sandy in parts and during the last war they cut steps to link the path with the flat rocks below for some reason. I won't take you out there, don't worry."

The sun disappeared beyond the rim of the world and the twilight began to gather beneath the red afterglow of the sky. They lingered for a while, both reluctant to leave the restless fascination of the sea, but in the end Jon led the way up the path back to the house. As they entered the driveway Marijohn came out to meet them, and Sarah wondered if she had been watching them from some vantage point upstairs as they walked up from the beach.

"Max phoned, Jon. He said you'd mentioned something about inviting him to Clougy for a day or two."

"God, so I did! When I dined with him in London he said he would have to go down to Cornwall to visit a maiden aunt at Bude or Newquay or one of those huge tourist towns up the coast, and I told him there was a remote possibility that I might be revisiting Clougy at about this time . . . What a bloody nuisance! I don't want Max breezing up in his latest sports car with some goddamned woman on the seat beside him. Did he leave his phone number?"

"Yes, he was speaking from Bude."

"Hell . . . I'd better invite him to dinner or something. No, that's not really very sociable—I suppose he'll have to stay the night. . . . No, damn it, why should he turn up here and use Clougy as a base for fornication? I had enough of that in the past."

"He may be alone."

"What, Max? Alone? Don't be ridiculous! Max wouldn't know what to do with himself unless he had some woman with him all the time!"

"He didn't mention a woman."

Jon stared. "Do you want him here?"

"You made the gesture of having dinner with him in London and renewing the friendship. He's obviously content to forget. If you made a semi-invitation to him to visit Clougy, then I don't see how you can turn round now and tell him to go to hell."

"I can do what I damn well like," said Jon. He

turned to Sarah. "I've told you about Max, haven't I? Would you be cross if he came to dinner tomorrow and spent the night?"

"No, darling, of course not. I'd like to meet him."

"All right, then. So be it." He turned aside and then glanced at her. "You go up to bed if you're tired. I won't be long. I'd better phone Max now while I still feel in a hospitable mood."

"All right," she said, glad of the excuse to go to bed, for she was by now feeling sleepy after the long journey followed by the long hours of sea air. "I'll go on up. Goodnight, Marijohn."

"Goodnight." The mouth smiled faintly. When Sarah paused at the top of the stairs to glance back into the hall, she saw that the woman was still watching her, but even as she stopped abruptly on the landing, Marijohn merely smiled again and moved into the livingroom to join Jon.

The door closed softly behind her.

Sarah still stood motionless at the top of the stairs. Two minutes elapsed, then a third. Suddenly, without knowing the reason but moving through instinct, she padded softly back downstairs and tiptoed across the hall until she was standing outside the door of the drawing-room.

Jon wasn't on the phone.

"There's only one thing that puzzles me," she heard him say, and her cheeks were hot with shame as she stood eavesdropping on their conversation. "And that's the anonymous phone call I had on my arrival in London, the call saying I'd killed Sophia. I still don't understand who it could have been. It must have been either Michael or Max or Eve, but why didn't they follow it up with something definite such as blackmail? It doesn't make sense."

There was a long pause. And then Jon said sharply: "What do you mean?"

"I tried to tell you before dinner when we were all having drinks."

Another silence. Then: "No," said Jon. "I don't believe it. It couldn't have been. You don't mean—"

"Yes," said Marijohn quietly from far away. "It was Justin."

II

The sound of the piano drifted from the house and floated up the cliff path which led north to Cape Cornwall and Zennor Head. Justin's knowledge of classical music was adequate but not exceptional; he could not name the title of the Mozart composition.

He was just gathering his painting gear together and stowing it neatly in his canvas bag when below him he heard the music stop and then far away the distant click of a latch as the French windows into the garden opened. He paused, straining his eyes in the gathering dusk, and saw a figure leave the shadow of the rhododendrons and stop to scan the hillside.

Automatically, without hesitation, Justin stepped behind a rock.

Footsteps sounded faintly, growing louder with every second. Justin scowled at his painting gear, shoved it behind a boulder and sat down waiting, his eyes watching the night darken the sea. He didn't have to wait very long.

"Ah, there you are," said Jon easily, stepping out of the darkness. "I thought you might be up here. Have you been painting?"

"No, I went for a walk." He stared out to sea, as his

father sat down beside him on the long rock and took out a cigarette case.

"Justin, if I ask you an honest question will you try and give me an honest answer?"

The sea was a dark motionless pool, the surf distant flecks of gray. "Of course," said Justin politely, and felt the sweat begin to moisten his palms.

"Does this place remind you too much of your mother?"

"My mother?" His voice was untroubled, vaguely surprised, but his eyes didn't see the view before him any more, only the bowl of cherries long ago and the woman's voice saying indulgently, "But you'll get so *fat,* Justin!" He cleared his throat. "Yes, it does remind me of her from time to time. But not enough to matter. I'm glad I came back because it was like coming home after a long time abroad."

"You were very fond of your mother, weren't you?"

Justin said nothing.

"I didn't realize," said Jon, "that you blamed me for her death."

Horror ebbed through Justin in dark suffocating waves. Putting his hands palm downwards on either side of his thighs, he clasped the ridge of rock and stared blindly down at the dusty path beneath his feet.

"What happened, Justin?" said his father's voice gently. "Why did you think I'd murdered her? Did you overhear something? Did you see us quarrel once when we didn't know you were there?"

He managed to shake his head.

"Then why?"

"I—" He shrugged his shoulders, glad of the darkness which hid his tears. "I—I don't know."

"But there must be some reason. You wouldn't have made the phone call unless there was some reason."

"I hated you because I thought you hadn't written and because I thought you were going to pass through London without bothering to contact me. It—it doesn't matter now." He took a deep breath, filling his lungs with the sea air. "I'm sorry," he whispered, the apology little more than a sigh. "I didn't mean it."

The man was silent, thinking.

"How did you know about the call?" said Justin suddenly. "How did you know it was me?"

"Marijohn guessed."

"But how did she know?"

"She says you are very like me and so she finds it easy to understand you."

"I don't see how she can possibly understand." He clasped the ridge of rock a little tighter. "And I'm not like you at all."

There was silence.

"When I was ten," said Jon, "my father paid one of his rare visits to London. The news of his arrival was in the evening paper because the expedition had received a certain amount of publicity, and my mother spent the entire evening saying she was quite sure he wouldn't bother to come and see me. So, just out of interest, I sent a telegram to his hotel saying I was dead, and sat back to watch the results. I expect you can imagine what happened—complete chaos. My mother wept all over the house saying she couldn't think who could have been so cruel as to play such a dreadful practical joke, and my father without hesitation took me by the scruff of the neck and nearly belted the life out of me. I never forgave him for that beating; if he hadn't neglected me for years at a time I wouldn't have sent the telegram, so in effect he was punishing me for his own sins."

Justin swallowed unevenly. "But you didn't neglect me."

"I did when you didn't answer my letters." He leaned back, slumping against another rock and drew heavily on his cigarette so that the glowing tip wavered in the darkness. "Justin, I have to know. Why did you think I'd killed your mother?"

"I—I knew she wasn't faithful to you." He leaned forward, closing his eyes for a moment in a supreme effort to explain his emotions of ten years ago. "I knew you quarreled, and it gradually became impossible for me to love you both any more. It was like a war in which one was forced to choose sides. And I chose your side because you always had time for me and you were strong and kind and I admired you more than anyone else in the world. So when she died, I—I didn't blame you, I only knew it was just and right, and so I never said a word to anyone, not even to you because I thought it was the best way showing my—my loyalty —that I was on your side. And then when you went away to Canada and I never heard from you again, I began to think I'd made the wrong judgment and gradually I grew to hate you enough to make that phone call when you came back to London." He stopped. Far away below them, the surf thudded dully on the single and the waves burst against the black cliffs.

"But Justin," said Jon, "I didn't kill your mother. It was an accident. You must believe that, because it's the truth."

Justin turned his head slowly to face him. There was a long silence.

"Why did you think I'd killed her, Justin?"

The night was still, the two men motionless beneath the dark skies. For a moment Justin had a long searing desire to tell the truth; and then the ingrained convictions of ten years made him cautious and he shrugged his shoulders vaguely before turning away to stare out to sea.

"I suppose," he said vaguely, "because I knew you were always quarreling and I felt you hated her enough to have pushed her to death. I was only a child, muddled and confused. I didn't really know anything at all."

Was it Justin's imagination or did his father seem to relax almost imperceptibly in relief? Justin's senses sharpened, his mind torn by doubts. In the midst of all his uncertainties he was aware of his brain saying very clearly: I must know. I can't let it rest now. I must find out the truth before I go away to Canada. Aloud he said: "Shall we go back to the house? I'm getting rather cold as I forgot to bring a sweater and Marijohn and Sarah will be wondering where we are . . ."

III

It was late when Jon came to the bedroom, and Sarah opening her eyes in the darkness, saw that the luminous hands of her clock pointed to half-past eleven. She waited, pretending to be asleep, and presently he slid into bed beside her and she felt his body brush lightly against her own. He sighed, sounding unexpectedly weary, and she longed to take him in her arms and say, "Jonny, why didn't you tell me about the anonymous phone call? You told me about the dreadful rumors which circulated after Sophia's death, so why not tell me about the call? And after Marijohn had said the caller was Justin, why did you go through to the other room to the piano and start playing that empty stilted rondo of Mozart's which I know perfectly well you dislike? And why did you say nothing else to Marijohn and she say nothing to you? The conversation should have begun then, not ended. It was all so strange and so puzzling, and I want so much to understand and help . . ."

But she said nothing, not liking to confess that she had eavesdropped on their conversation by creeping back downstairs and listening at the closed door, and presently Jon was breathing evenly beside her and the chance to talk to him was gone.

When she awoke the piano was playing again far away downstairs and the sun was slanting sideways through the curtains into the room. She sat up. It was after nine. As she went down the corridor she heard the sound of the piano more clearly and she realized with a shaft of uneasiness that he was again playing Mozart. After a quick bath she dressed in a pair of slacks and a shirt and went tentatively downstairs to the music room.

He was playing the minuet from the thirty-ninth symphony, lingering over the full pompous chords and the mincing quavers so that the arrangement bore the faint air of a burlesque.

"Hullo," she said lightly, moving into the room. "I thought you didn't like Mozart? You never played his music at home." She stopped to kiss the top of his head. "Why have you suddenly gone Mozart-mad?" And then she suddenly glanced over her shoulder and saw that Marijohn was watching them from the window-seat.

Jon yawned, decided to abandon classicial music altogether and began to play the Floyd Cramer arrangement of Hank Williams' "You Win Again." "Breakfast is ready and waiting for you, darling," he said leisurely. "Justin's in the diningroom and he'll show you where everything is."

"I see." She went out of the room slowly and made her way towards the diningroom; she felt baffled and ill-at-ease for a reason she could not define, and her uneasiness seemed to cast a shadow over the morning so that she started to feel depressed. She opened the diningroom door and decided that she didn't want much breakfast.

"Good morning," said Justin. "Did you sleep well?"

"Yes," she lied. "Very well."

"Cereal?"

"No, thank you. Just toast." She sat down, watching him pour out her coffee, and suddenly she remembered the conversation she had overheard the previous night and recalled that for some unknown reason Justin had anonymously accused Jon of murdering Sophia.

"Are you sure you wouldn't like a cooked breakfast?" he asked politely. "There are sausages and eggs on the hot plate."

"No, thank you."

The piano started to play again in the distance, abandoning the American country music and reverting to classical territory with a Chopin prelude.

"Are you going painting this morning, Justin?" she asked, her voice drowning the noise of the piano.

"Perhaps. I'm not sure." He glanced at her warily over the *Times* and then stirred his coffee with nonchalance. "Why?"

"I thought I might try some painting myself," she said, helping herself to marmalade. "I was going to consult you about the best views for a landscape watercolor."

"Oh, I see." He hesitated, uncertain. "What about my father?"

"It rather sounds as if he's going to have a musical morning."

"Yes," he said. "I suppose it does."

"Does Marijohn play the piano?"

"No, I don't think so."

"Oh . . . the piano seems very well-tuned."

"Yes," said Justin. "But then she knew he was coming."

"She didn't know for certain till yesterday afternoon!"

He stared at her. "Oh no, she knew a long while before that. She had a man up from Penzance to tune the piano last week."

The shaft of uneasiness was so intense that it hurt. Sarah took a large sip of her coffee to steady her nerves and then started to spread the marmalade over the buttered toast.

From somewhere far away the piano stopped. Footsteps echoed in the corridor and the next moment Jon was walking into the room.

"How are you this morning, darling?" he said, kissing her with a smile and then moving over to the window to glance out into the garden. "You hardly gave me a chance to ask just now. . . . What do you want to do today? Anything special?"

"Well, I thought I might paint this morning, but—"

"Fine," he said. "Get Justin to take you somewhere nice. Marijohn has shopping to do in Penzance and I've promised to drive her over in the car. You don't want to come to Penzance, do you? It'll be crammed with tourists at this time of year and much too noisy. You stay here and do just what you like." He swung ro to face her again, still smiling. "All right?"

"Yes . . . all right, Jon."

"Good! Look after her, Justin, and be on your best behavior." He moved to the door. "Marijohn?"

There was an answering call from the kitchen and he closed the door noisily behind him before moving off down the corridor to the back of the house.

Justin cleared his throat. "More coffee, Sarah?"

"No," she said. "No, thank you."

He stood up, easing back his chair delicately across the floor. "If you'll excuse me, I'll just go and assemble my painting gear. I won't be long. What time would you like to leave?"

"Oh . . . any time. Whenever you like."

"I'll let you know when I'm ready, then," he said and padded out of the room towards the hall.

She lingered a long time over the breakfast table before going upstairs to extract her paintbox and board from one of her suitcases. Jon called her from the hall just as she was pausing to tidy her hair.

"We're just off now, darling—sure you'll be all right?"

"Yes, I'm almost ready myself."

"Have a good time!"

She sat listening to the closing doors, the quick roar of the engine bursting into life, the crunch of the tires on the gravel, and then the sound of the car faded in the distance and she was alone. She went downstairs. In the drawing-room she found Justin waiting, studiously reading the *Times*, scrupulously dressed in the best English tailored casual clothes, but still managing to look like a foreigner.

"I don't know which way you'd like to go," he said. "We could take Marijohn's car and drive south to Sennen and Land's End, or north to Kenidjack Castle and Cape Cornwall. The views from the cliff out over the ruined mines of Kenidjack are good to paint." He paused, waiting for her comment, and when she nodded he said politely, "Would you care to go that way?"

"Yes, that sounds fine."

They set off, not speaking much, and drove north along the main road to the crossroads beyond St. Just where the left fork took them towards the sea to the mine workings of Kenidjack. At the end of the road high up on the cliffs they parked the car and started walking and scrambling over the hillside to the best view of the surrounding scenery. Below them the sea was a rich blue, shot with green patches near the off-shore rocks, and there was no horizon. As the cliff path wound steeply above the rocks the great cliffs of Kendijack and the withered stones of the old mine workings rose ahead of them, and Sarah saw that the light was perfect. When she sat down at last, gasping after the climb, she felt the excitement quicken within her as she gazed over the shimmering view before her eyes.

"I've bought some lemonade and some biscuits," said Justin, modestly demonstrating his presence of mind. "It's hot walking."

They sat down and drank some lemonade in silence.

"It would be nice for a dog up here," said Sarah after a while. "All the space in the world to run and chase rabbits."

"We used to have a dog. It was a sheepdog called Flip, short for Philip, after the Duke of Edinburgh. My mother, like many foreigners, loved all the royal family."

"Oh." She broke off a semi-circle of biscuit and looked at it with unseeing eyes. "And what happened to Flip?"

"My mother had him put to sleep because he tore one of her best cocktail dresses to shreds. I cried all night. There was a row, I think, when my father came home." He reached for his canvas bag and took out his painting book absentmindedly. "I don't feel much like doing watercolors this morning. Perhaps I'll do a char-coal sketch and then work up a picture in oils later when I get home."

"Can I see some of your paintings?"

He paused, staring at a blank page. "You won't like them."

"Why not?"

"They're rather peculiar. I've never dared show them to anyone except Marijohn, and of course she's quite different."

"Why?" said Sarah. "I mean, why is Marijohn different?"

"Well, she is, isn't she? She's not like other people. . . . This is a watercolor of the cove—you probably won't recognize it. And this—"

Sarah drew in her breath sharply. He stopped, his face suddenly scarlet, and stared down at his toes.

The painting was a mass of greens and grays, the sky torn by stormclouds, the rocks dark and jagged, like some monstrous animal in a nightmare. The composition was jumbled and unskilled, but the savage power and sense of beauty were unmistakable. Sarah thought of Jon playing Rachmaninoff. If Jon could paint, she thought, this is the type of picture he would produce.

"It's very good, Justin," she said honestly. "I'm not sure that I like it, but it's unusual and striking. Can you show me some more?"

He showed her three more, talking in a low, hesitant voice, the tips of his ears pink with pleasure.

"When did you first start painting?"

"Oh, long ago . . . when I went to public school, I suppose. But it's just a hobby. Figures are my real interest."

"Figures?"

"Math—calculations—odds. Anything involving figures. That's why I started with an insurance firm in the City, but it was pretty boring and I hated the routine of nine till five."

"I see," she said, and thought of Jon talking of his own first job in the city, Jon saying, "God, it was boring! Christ, the routine!"

Justin was fidgeting with a stick of charcoal, edging a black square on the cover of his paint book. Even his restlessness reminded her of Jon.

"You're not a bit as I imagined you would be," he said unexpectedly without looking up. "You're very different from the sort of people who used to come down here to Clougy."

"And very different from your mother too, I expect," she said levelly, watching him.

"Oh yes," he said, completely matter-of-fact. "Of course." He found a clean page in his book and drew a line with his stick of charcoal. "My mother had no interests or hobbies, like painting or music. She used to get so bored, and the weekend parties were her main interest in life. My father didn't really want them. Sometimes he and I used to walk down to the Flat Rocks just to get away from all the people—but she used to revel in entertaining guests, dreaming up exotic menus and planning midnight swimming parties in the cove."

"There were guests staying here when she died, weren't there?"

"Yes, that's right." He drew another charcoal line. "But no one special. Uncle Max drove down from London and arrived on Friday evening. He had a new car which he enjoyed showing off and boasting about as soon as he arrived, but it really was a lovely thing. He took me for a ride in it, I remember. . . . Have you met Uncle Max yet?"

"No, not yet."

"He was fun," said Justin. "He and my father used to laugh a lot together. But my mother thought he was rather boring. She was never interested in any man unless he was good-looking and was always bitchy to any woman who didn't look like the back end of a bus. . . . Uncle Max was very ugly. Not that it mattered. He always had plenty of girlfriends. My parents used to play a game whenever they knew he was coming down—it was called the Who-Will-Max-Produce-This-Time, and they used to try to guess what she would look like. The girl was always different each time, of course. . . . During that last weekend they played the game on the morning before Max arrived and bet each other he would turn up with a petite redhead with limpid blue eyes. They were so cross when he turned up with a statuesque blonde, very slim and tall and elegant. She was called Eve. I didn't like her at all because she never took any notice of me the entire weekend."

He closed the paintbook, produced a pair of sunglasses and leaned back against the grassy turf to watch the blue sky far above. "Then Uncle Michael came down with Marijohn. They'd been in Cornwall on business, I think, and they arrived together at Clougy just in time for dinner. Uncle Michael was Marijohn's husband. I always called him Uncle, although I never called her Aunt . . . I don't know why. He was nice, too, but utterly different from Uncle Max. He was the sort of person you see on suburban trains in the rush-hour reading the law report in the *Times*. Sometimes he used to play French cricket with me on the lawn after tea. . . . And then were was Marijohn." He paused. "To be honest, I never liked her much when I was small, probably because I always felt she was never very interested in me. It's different now, of course—she's been so kind to me during the past fortnight, and I've become very fond of her. But ten years ago . . . I think she was really only interested in my father at the time. Nobody else liked her except him, you see. Uncle Max always seemed to want to avoid being alone with her, Eve the statuesque blonde, never seemed to find a word to say to her, and my mother naturally resented her because Marijohn was much more beautiful than she was. And Uncle Michael . . . no, I'd forgotten Uncle Michael. It was obvious he loved her. He kissed her in public and gave her special smiles—oh God, you know! The sort of thing you notice and squirm at when you're a small boy. . . . So there they all were at Clougy on Friday evening, and twenty-four hours later my mother was dead."

The sea murmured far away; gulls soared, borne aloft by the warm breeze.

"Was it a successful party?" Sarah heard herself say tentatively at last.

"Successful?" said Justin, propping himself upon one elbow to stare at her. "Successful? It was dreadful! Everything went wrong from start to finish. Uncle Max quarreled with the statuesque blonde—they had an awful row after breakfast on Saturday and she went and locked herself in her room. I've no idea what the row was about. Then when Uncle Max went to his car to work off his anger by driving, my mother wanted him to take her to St. Ives to get some fresh shellfish for dinner; but my father didn't want her to go so there was another row. In the end my father went off to the Flat Rocks and took me with him. It was terrible. He didn't speak a word the entire time. After a while Marijohn came and my father sent me back to the house to find out when lunch would be ready. We had a maid help at Clougy in those days to do the mid-day cooking when there were guests. When I got back to the house I found Uncle Michael looking for Marijohn so I told him to go down to the Flat Rocks. After I'd found out about the lunch and stopped for elevenses I started off back again, but I met my father on his own coming back from the cliff path and he took me back to the house and started to play the piano. He played for a long time. In the end I got bored and slipped back to the kitchen to inquire about lunch again. I was always hungry in those days. . . . And then Uncle Michael and Marijohn came back and shut themselves in the drawing-room. I tried listening at the key-hole but I couldn't hear anything, and anyway my father found me listening and was cross enough to slap me very hard across the seat of my trousers so I scuttled down to the cove out of the way after that. My mother and Uncle Max didn't come back for lunch and Eve stayed in her room. I had to take a tray up to her and leave it outside the door, but when I came to collect it an hour later it hadn't been touched so I sat down at the top of the stairs and ate it myself. I didn't think anyone would mind. . . .

"My mother and Uncle Max came back in time for tea. I was rather frightened, I think, because for some reason I expected my father to have the most almighty row with her, but—" He stopped pulling up grass with his fingers, his eyes staring out to sea.

"But what?"

"But nothing happened," said Justin slowly. "It was most odd. I can't quite describe how odd it was. My father was playing the piano and Marijohn was with him, I remember. Uncle Michael had gone fishing. And absolutely nothing happened. . . . After tea Uncle Max and my mother went down to the cove for a bathe, and still nothing happened. I followed them down to the beach but my mother told me to go away, so I walked along the shore till I found Uncle Michael fishing. We talked for a while. Then I went back and snatched some supper from the larder as I wasn't sure whether I'd be dining with the grown-ups or not. As it happened I was, but I didn't want to be hungry. Then Eve came downstairs, asking for Uncle Max and when I told her he'd gone swimming with my mother she walked off towards the cove.

"Dinner was at eight. It was delicious, one of my mother's best fish-dishes, fillet of sole garnished with lobster and crab and shrimps. . . . I had three helpings. I particularly remember because no one else ate at all. Eve had gone back to her room again, I believe, so that just left Max, Michael, Marijohn and my parents. My mother made most of the conversation but after a while she seemed bewildered and didn't talk so much. And then—" He stopped again, quite motionless, the palms of his hands flat against the springy turf.

"Yes?"

"And then Marijohn and my father started to talk. They talked about music mostly. I didn't understand a word of what they were saying and I don't think anyone else did either. At last my mother told me to go to bed and I said I'd help with the washing-up—my usual dodge for avoiding bed, as I used to walk into the kitchen and straight out of the back door—but she wouldn't hear of it. In the end it was Uncle Michael who took me upstairs, and when we stood up from the dinner table, everyone else rose as well and began to filter away. The last thing I remember as I climbed the stairs and looked back into the hall was my father putting on a red sweater as if he was going out. Uncle Michael said to me: 'What are you looking at?' and I couldn't tell him that I was wondering if my father was going out for a walk to the Flat Rocks and whether

I could slip out and join him when everyone thought I was in bed. . . . But Uncle Michael was with me too long, and I never had the chance. He read me a chapter of *Treasure Island* which I thought was rather nice of him. However, when I was alone, I lay awake for a long time, wondering what was going on, and listening to the gramaphone in the music room below. It was an orchestral record, a symphony, I think. After a while it stopped. I thought: maybe he's going down now to the Flat Rocks. So I got out of bed and pulled on a pair of shorts and pullover and my sand shoes. When I glanced out of the window, I saw a shadow move out of the driveway and so I slipped out to follow him.

"It was rather spooky in the moonlight. I remember being frightened, especially when I saw someone coming up the path from the beach towards me and I had to hide behind a rock. It was Eve. She was breathing hard as if she'd been running and her face was streaked with tears. She didn't see me."

He was silent, fingering the short grass, and after a while he took off his sunglasses and she saw his dark eyes had a remote, withdrawn expression.

"I went up the cliff path a long way, but he was always too far ahead for me to catch him up and the sea would have drowned my voice if I'd called out. In the end I had to pause to get my breath, and when I looked back I saw someone was following me. I was really scared then. I dived into a sea of bracken and buried myself as deep as I could. Presently the other person went by."

A pause. Around them lay the tranquillity of the summer morning, the calm sea, the still sky, the quiet cliffs.

"Who was it?" said Sarah at last.

Another pause. The scene was effortlessly beautiful. Then: "My mother," said Justin. "I never saw her again."

Three

I

WHEN THEY ARRIVED back at Clougy they found the car standing in the drive but the house was empty and still. In the kitchen something was cooking in the oven and two saucepans simmered gently on the stove; on the table was a square of paper covered with a clear printed writing.

"Justin!" called Sarah.

He was upstairs putting his painting gear away. "Hullo?"

"Marijohn wants you to go up to the farm to get some milk." She replaced the note absently beneath the rolling pin and wandered out into the hall just as he came downstairs to join her. "I wonder where they are," she said to him as he stopped to check how much money he had in his pockets. "Do you think they've gone down to the beach for a stroll before lunch?"

"Probably." He apparently decided he had enough money to buy the milk, and moved over to the front door. "Do you want to come up to the farm?"

"No, I'll go down to the beach to meet them and tell them we're back."

He nodded and stepped out into the sunshine of the

drive. The gravel crunched beneath his feet as he walked away out of the gate and up the track to the farm.

After he had gone, Sarah followed him to the gate and took the path which led down into the cove, but presently she stopped to listen. It was very still. Far away behind her she could still hear the faint rush of the stream as it tumbled past the disused waterwheel. But apart from that there was nothing, only the calm of a summer morning and the bare rock-strewn hills on either side of her. London seemed a thousand miles away.

Presently the path forked, one turning leading up on to the cliffs, the other descending into the cove. She walked on slowly downhill, and suddenly the sound of the sea was in her ears and a solitary gull was swooping overhead with a desolate empty cry, and the loneliness seemed to increase for no apparent reason. At the head of the beach she paused to scan the rocks but there was no sign of either Jon or his cousin and presently she started to climb uphill to meet the cliff path in order to gain a better view of the cove.

The tide was out; the rocks stretched far into the sea. She moved further along the path round the side of the hill until presently, almost before she had realized it, the cove was hidden from her and the path was threading its way through the heather along the shallow cliff.

And below were the rocks. Hundreds of thousands of rocks. Vast boulders, gigantic slabs, small blocks of stone all tumbled at the base of the cliff and frozen in a jagged pattern as if halted by some invisible hand on their race into the sea.

The path forked again, one branch leading straight on along the same level, the other sloping downhill to the cliff's edge.

Sarah stopped.

Below her the rocks formed a different pattern. They were larger, smoother, flatter, descending in a series of levels to the waves far below. There were little inlets, all reflecting the blue sky, and the waves of the outgoing tide were gentle and calm as they washed effortlessly over the rocky shelves and through the seaweed lagoons.

It was then that she saw Jon's red shirt. It lay stretched out on a rock to dry beneath the hot sunshine, and as she strained her eyes to make sure she was not mistaken, she could see the pebbles weighting the sleeves to prevent the soft breeze from blowing it back into the water.

She moved on down the path to the cliff's edge. The cliff was neither very steep nor very high but she had to pause all the same to consider how she was going to scramble down. She saw the rough steps, but one was missing and another seemed to be loose; the sand around them bore no trace of footmarks to indicate that it would be easy enough to find another way down. She stood among the heather, her glance searching the cliff's edge, and suddenly she realized she was frightened and angry and puzzled. This was where Sophia had died. The steps were the ones leading down the cliff and the rocks below were the Flat Rocks. And Jon had come back. He had come back deliberately to the very spot where his wife had been killed. Marijohn had taken him. It was her fault. If he had not wanted to see her again he wouldn't have dreamed of returning to Clougy. He had talked of how fond he was of the place and how much he wanted to see it again in spite of all that had happened, but it had been a lie. He had come back to see Marijohn, not for any other reason.

She sat down suddenly in the heather, her cheeks

burning, the scene blurring before her eyes. But why, her brain kept saying, trying to be sensible and reasonable. Why? Why am I crying? Why do I feel sick and miserable? Why am I suddenly so convinced that Jon came back here not because he loved Clougy but solely because of his cousin? And why should it matter even if he did? Why shouldn't he be fond of his cousin? Am I jealous? Why am I so upset? Why, why, why?

Because Jon lied to me. He had planned this trip before he ever mentioned it to me—and Marijohn had the piano tuned because she knew he was coming.

Because he talks to Marijohn of things which he has never mentioned to me.

Because this morning he preferred Marijohn's company to mine . . .

She dashed away her tears, pressing her lips together in a determined effort to pull herself together. She was being absurd, worse than an adolescent. Trust was a basic element of marriage, and she trusted Jon. Everything was perfectly all right and she was imagining all kinds of dreadful possibilities without a grain of proof. She would go down to the rocks to meet them because there was no reason why she should be afraid of what she might find and because it was utterly ridiculous to sit on top of a cliff weeping. She would go right away.

She found a way to the first shelf after a few minutes and started to scramble over towards the red shirt. In spite of herself she found she was thinking about Marijohn again. Marijohn wasn't like other people, Justin had said. Marijohn could talk to Jon when he was in the Distant Mood. She could cope with him when Sarah did not even begin to know how to deal with the situation. Marijohn . . .

The scramble over the rocks was more difficult than

128

it had appeared from the cliff path above. She found herself making wide detours and after a time she had lost sight of the red shirt and realized she had been forced to move too far over to the left.

It was then that she heard Jon laugh.

She stopped, her heart thumping from the exertion of the scramble and from something else which she refused to acknowledge. Then, very slowly, despising herself for the subterfuge, she moved forward quietly, taking great care that she should see them before they should see her.

She suddenly realized she was very frightened indeed.

There was a large white rock ahead, its surface worn smooth by centuries of wind and rain. It was cold beneath her hot hands. She moved forward, still gripping the rock, and edged herself sideways until she could see round it to the rocks beyond.

Relief rushed through her in great warm overwhelming waves.

Beyond her was a small lagoon, similar to the ones she had seen from the cliff-path, and a flat ledge of rock sloped gently to the water's edge. Marijohn was lying on her back on the rocks enjoying the sunshine. She wore a white bathing costume and dark glasses which were tilted to the edge of her nose and as she gazed up at the blue sky far above her, her arms were behind her head, the palms of her hands pillowing her hair.

Jon, in black bathing trunks, was sitting by the water's edge some distance away from her and was paddling his feet idly in the still water of the lagoon.

Sarah was just about to call out to him and move out from behind the rock when Jon laughed again and splashed one foot lazily in the water.

Marijohn sat up slowly, propping herself on one elbow and took off her sunglasses. Sarah couldn't see her face, only the back of her shining hair and the smooth tanned skin above the edge of her bathing costume.

"Why?" she said. She said nothing else at all, only the one monosyllable, and Sarah wondered what she meant and what she was querying.

Jon swiveled round, and Sarah instinctively withdrew behind the white boulder so that he would not see her.

"I don't know," she heard him say uneasily. "There's no reason why I should feel so happy."

"I know."

There was a silence. When Sarah had the courage to look at them again she saw that Jon was standing up, looking out to sea and that although Marijohn was also standing up she was still several paces away from him.

They were motionless.

The sea lapped insistently at the rocks beyond the lagoon; a wave broke into the pool and the spray began to fly as the tide turned. Nothing else happened. There was no reason at all why suddenly Sarah should feel aware of panic. And as she stood rigid with fear, hardly able to breathe, she heard Jon say quietly to his cousin, "Why don't you come to Canada?"

There was a pause. Everything seemed to cease except the sea. Then: "My dear Jon, what on earth would be the point of that?"

"I don't know," he said, and he sounded strangely lost and baffled. "I don't know."

"We've been into all this before, Jon."

"Yes," he said emptily. "We've been into all this before."

"After your wife was dead and my marriage was in ruins we went into it in detail right here at Clougy."

"For God's sake!" he shouted suddenly. "For God's

sake don't talk of that scene with Sophia again! Christ Almighty—"

"Jon, darling."

And still they stood apart from one another, he slumped against a rock, his hands tight, white fists at his sides, she motionless by the water's edge, the sun shining full on her hair.

"Marijohn," he said, "I know we've never, never mentioned this in words either now after I met you again or ten years after it all happened, but—"

"There's no need to mention it," she said swiftly. "I understand. There's no need to talk about it."

"But . . . oh God, why? Why, Marijohn? Why, why, why?"

She stared at him, still motionless, but somehow that strange stillness was lost as if a spell had been broken and the mystery of the quiet scene was shattered.

She doesn't understand him, thought Sarah suddenly. She's going to have to ask him what he means.

And somehow the knowledge was a victory which she could neither understand nor explain.

"Yes," said Jon. "Why? Why did you have to kill Sophia?"

A wave thudded against the rocks and exploded in a cloud of spray so that the lagoon was no longer still and peaceful but a turmoil of boiling surf. And after the roar of the undertow had receded came a faint shout from the cliff high above them, and Sarah saw Justin standing on the top of the cliffs waving to attract their attention.

She drew further out of sight at once so that he wouldn't see her, and began to scramble back over the rocks to find a hiding-place before the others started to retrace their steps to the cliff path. When she eventually sank down to rest behind a pile of boulders her breath was coming in gasps which hurt her lungs, and her whole body was trembling with the shock. She sat there numbly for a while, and then the tide began to surge across the rocks towards her as it ate its way greedily inland to the cliffs, and she knew she would have to go back.

Moving very slowly, she stood up and began to stumble blindly back towards the cliff path to Clougy.

II

When Justin returned from the farm with the milk he met the postman pushing his bicycle up the track from Clougy and they paused for a moment to talk to one another.

"Only two letters today," said the Cornishman placidly, extracting a large handkerchief to mop his forehead. "One for Mrs. Rivers, t'other for yourself. Lor' it's hot today, ain't it! Makes a change, I say. Too much rain lately."

Justin agreed politely.

Presently when he reached the house he put the milk down on the hall table and stopped to examine the mail. The letter to Marijohn was postmarked London, the address typewritten. Perhaps it was from Michael Rivers' office. Rivers, Justin knew, still handled Marijohn's legal affairs.

The other envelope was white and square and covered by a large level handwriting which he did not recognize, *J. Towers, Esq.*, the writer had scrawled, *Clougy, St. Just, Penzance, Cornwall.* The post-mark was also London.

Justin fumbled with the flap of the envelope, wondering who could be writing to him. The sensation of puzzled interest was pleasant and when he pulled the single sheet of white paper from the close-fitting envelope he sat down on the stairs before opening the folded slip of paper to see the signature.

The signature was very short. Only three letters. Someone had merely written *Eve* in that same large level handwriting, but even as he realized with a jolt that the letter wasn't meant for him his glance travelled to the top of the paper automatically.

Dear Jon, Eve had written. *Had dinner with Max in London last week. He wanted to know why you had asked him where I lived and why you had sounded so interested in me. We ended up by having a long talk about that time ten years ago, and in the end he told me you were back at Clougy and that he had decided to come down and see you. Just thought I'd drop you a line to warn you to be pretty damn careful, as he knows more than you think. If you're interested in hearing more about this, why don't you come and see me any time from Saturday onwards—address and phone number above. I'm staying in St. Ives for a few days and won't be going back to town till Tuesday. Eve.*

Justin read the letter three times. Then, very carefully, he replaced the sheet of notepaper in its neat white envelope and tucked the letter deep into the privacy of his wallet.

III

When Sarah reached the house at last there was a silver-gray Rolls Royce in the driveway and the sound of laughter floated from the open windows of the drawing-room towards her on the still air. She slipped into the house by the sidedoor and managed to creep up to her room without being seen. Sitting down in front of the dressing-table she stared into the mirror for one long moment before fumbling with the jars of make-up, and then she stood up blindly and moved into the bathroom to wash the tearstains from her face. When she came back to the dressing-table Jon was on the lawn below and calling something over his shoulder.

". . . imagine what can have happened to her," she heard him say. "Are you sure she said she was going down to the cove, Justin?"

She could not hear Justin's reply. She stood by the window shielded by the curtain and watched Jon as he began to move forward again across the lawn.

". . . better go and find her in case she's got lost . . ." His voice tailed away and presently she found her view of him was blurring before her eyes until she could scarcely see.

She sat down again at the dressing-table.

"Of course she's not lost," Marijohn's voice said clearly from the lawn below, sounding surprisingly close at hand. "She's probably gone for a walk before lunch."

"Another walk?" said a man's unfamiliar drawl, sounding amused. "God, she must be an Amazon! No normal woman would spend the morning toiling up the cliffs at Kendijack and then toiling over some more cliffs around Clougy for a pre-prandial stroll! Jon never told me he'd married one of these keen outdoor types."

"He hasn't," said Marijohn briefly. "She's not."

"Thank God for that! I had a sudden hideous vision of a hearty female with muscular shoulders and tombstone teeth. . . . What's she like? Is she pretty? Jon said that physically she was just like Sophia."

"Justin," said Marijohn to the room behind her. "Would you—"

"He's gone. He slipped out a second ago when I

was making my anti-Amazon speech. Well, tell me about Sarah, Marijohn. Is she—"

"You'll meet her soon enough."

"Is Jon very much in love with her?"

"He married her."

"Yes, I know. I was very surprised. She must be damn good."

"Good?"

"In bed. Can I have another drink?"

"Of course."

There was a pause, the stillness of a hot summer morning.

"And you," said Max Alexander. "You. I'm surprised you never married again. What happened after the divorce? Did you go abroad? I never saw you in London."

"I worked in Paris for a while."

"God, that sounds glamorous!"

"It was extremely boring. I could only endure it for a year."

"And then?"

"I came back. Do you want some ice in your drink?"

"No, no, I can't bear this American fetish of loading every drink with ice. . . . Thanks . . . I see. And what did you do when you returned?"

"Nothing special."

"Did you come back here?"

"Not straight away."

"Lord, it's strange coming back! Didn't it seem strange to you?"

"No, why should it?"

"Why should it?"

"Yes, why should it? Clougy has many happy memories for me."

"You're not serious, of course."

"Perfectly. Why shouldn't I be?"

"Oh."

Another pause. A gull drifted far overhead, its wings outstretched, its neck craning towards the sun.

"I must say," said Max Alexander, "I never thought Jon would come back here, least of all with his new wife. Does he ever speak of Sophia?"

"Never."

"He's closed the door, as it were, on that part of his past?"

"Why do you suppose he asked you down here?"

"I was hoping," said Alexander, "that you could tell me."

"I'm not sure I quite understand you."

"No? Hell, Jon was crazy about Sophia, wasn't he? Any husband would have been. With a woman like that—"

"Sophia no longer exists. Jon's made a new life for himself and Sophia's memory is nothing to him now. Nothing at all."

"Yet he's married someone who physically and sexually—"

"Men often prefer one type of looks in a woman. It means nothing at all. Besides there's more to love than merely a sexual relationship or a physical attraction."

"That *is* the common delusion, I believe."

"You think any relationship between a man and a woman is basically sexual?"

"Of course it is! It's impossible for a man and a woman to have an intimate relationship with no sex in it whatsoever!"

"I think," said Marijohn, "we've somehow succeeded in wandering from the point."

"But don't you agree with me?"

"Agree with you? What am I supposed to be agreeing with?"

136

"That it's impossible for a man and a woman to have an intimate relationship with no sex in it whatsoever."

"That would depend upon the man and woman."

"On the contrary I'd say it depended entirely on their sexual capacity! Take Jon for instance. He's married twice and had a lot of women but no woman's going to interest him unless she attracts him physically."

"Why shouldn't Jon have his share of sex? Most men need it and get it so why shouldn't he? And why should his 'sexual capacity,' as you call it, affect any other relationship he might have? And what's so special about sex anyway? It often has nothing whatsoever to do with real intimacy. Why talk of it as if it were the beginning and end of everything? Sex is so often nothing but pointless futility."

Alexander hesitated slightly before he laughed. The hesitation made the laughter sound a little uncertain.

"For pointless futility it certainly seems to be doing very well!" And when she didn't answer he said easily, "That sounds very much a woman's point of view, Marijohn."

"Perhaps," she said flatly, not arguing, her footsteps moving into the house. "I must go and see how burnt the lunch is getting. Excuse me."

"Of course."

There was silence. Sarah found she was still clutching the edge of the dressing-table stool. She glanced into the mirror. Her dark eyes stared back at her, her dark hair straggling untidily from its position, her mouth unsmiling, devoid of make-up. She reached automatically for her lipstick.

I want to go, she thought; please, Jon, let's go—let's go anywhere so long as it's somewhere far from this place. Let's go now. If only I could go. . . .

She started to re-apply her powder.

I don't want to meet Max. I don't care if he was your friend once, Jon; I don't want to meet him because I can't bear men who talk of women and sex in bored amused voices as if they've seen all there is to see and know all there is to know. I want to go, Jon, now, this minute. If only we could go. . . .

She undid her hair and let it fall to her shoulders before brushing it upwards again and picking up her comb.

And most of all, Jon, I want to go away from your cousin because she doesn't like me, Jon, I know she doesn't, and I hate her, no matter how hard I try to pretend I don't. . . . I hate her and I'm afraid of her although I don't know why, and Jon, can't we go soon, Jon, because I want to escape. . . . It's not just because she dislikes me—in fact "dislike" is the wrong word. She despises me. You won't believe she despises me, Jon, because she's always been so kind to me ever since we set foot in this house, but she does, I know she does, because I can feel it. She despises me just as she despised Sophia.

She put down her comb and examined the little jar of liquid eye-shadow.

Better not to think of Sophia.

But all those lies. Jon, all those lies. And you swore to me her death was an accident. You lied and lied and lied for Marijohn. . . .

Oh, God, I want to go, I want to get away. Please Jon, take me away from this place because I'm frightened and I want to escape. . . .

She went out into the corridor. It was cool there, and the bannister was smooth against her hot palm. She walked downstairs, crossed the hall and entered the drawing-room.

The man turned as she came in. He turned to face her and she saw all that she had not seen when she had listened to his conversation earlier—the humorous mouth, the wide blue eyes that for some reason seemed very honest and trusting, the broken nose, the traces of plastic surgery which stretched from his left temple to the jawbone. There were lines about the mouth. They were deep lines which would get deeper with time, but apart from this there was no other indication that he had suffered and known pain. He looked older than Jon, but not much older. The suffering hadn't aged him, as it would have aged some men, nor had it given him the worn, tired appearance of exhaustion.

She stood staring, suddenly at a loss for words. It was some seconds before she realized that he too was experiencing difficulty in choosing his opening remarks.

"Good Lord!" he said at last, and his blue eyes were wide with honest surprise. "But you're young! I thought you were Jon's age. No one ever told me you were young."

She smiled awkwardly. "Not as young as all that!"

He smiled too, not saying anything, his eyes still faintly astonished, and she wondered what he was thinking and whether she was as like Sophia, as he had imagined she would be. "Where's Jon?" she said, for lack of anything else to say.

"He went out to look for you, as a matter of fact."

"Did he? I must have just missed him." She helped herself to a cigarette and he gave her a light. "When did you arrive?"

"About half an hour ago. Justin was the only one at home so he went down to the cove to tell everyone I'd arrived. Apparently I wasn't expected to lunch. . . . Jon tells me you're both going over to see some old friends of his in Penzance this afternoon?"

"Are we? I mean—" She blushed and laughed. "I

139

haven't seen Jon since breakfast. He and Marijohn went into Penzance this morning to do some shopping—"

"Ah, he must have arranged something when he was over there. . . . I was just wondering what I could do with myself while you're out. Marijohn says uncompromisingly that she has 'things to do' and Justin is taking her car to go over to St. Ives for some reason, so I'll be on my own. Maybe I'll have a swim or a paddle, depending on how Spartan I feel. I never usually bathe except in the Mediterranean. . . . Ah, here's Jon! He must have decided you hadn't lost yourself after all. . . . Jon!" He moved out through the open French windows on to the lawn beyond, his arm raised in greeting, and when he next spoke she heard the hard careless edge return to his voice. "Jon, why didn't you tell me how young and pretty your new wife is?"

IV

"I don't want to go," she said to Jon. "Would it matter awfully if I didn't come? I feel so tired."

The bedroom was quiet, shadowed by the Venetian blinds.

"Just as you like," said Jon. "I happened to meet this fellow when I was in Penzance this morning—I used to do a certain amount of business with him in the old days. When he invited us over this afternoon for a spin in his motor-boat, I thought it would be the sort of invitation you'd enjoy."

"I—I'm sorry, Jon."

"Of course you must rest if you're tired. Don't worry." He stooped to kiss her on the forehead. "Perhaps Marijohn will come," he said presently. "I'll ask her."

"She told Max she was going to be very busy this afternoon."

"That was probably merely a polite way of excusing herself from entertaining him. I'll see what she says." He turned to go.

"Jon, if you don't want to go alone, I'll—"

"No, no," he said. "You lie down and rest. That's much the most important thing. But I'll have to go over and see this fellow and his new motor-boat—I've committed myself. If Marijohn doesn't want to come I'll go alone."

So she waited upstairs in misery as he went down to talk with Marijohn, but when he came back she heard that Marijohn had decided against going with him.

"I'll be back around six," he said, kissing her again before he left the room. "Sleep well."

But she did not sleep. Presently she dressed, putting on slacks and a shirt and went downstairs. Justin had gone off to St. Ives and Marijohn was relaxing on the swing-seat in the garden with some unanswered correspondence and a pen. Alexander was nowhere to be seen.

In order that Marijohn would not see her, Sarah left the house by the back door and moved through the back gate on to the hillside behind the house. Five minutes later she was by the beach of the cove.

Alexander wasn't paddling. He had taken off his shirt to bask in the heat and eased off his shoes but he was sitting on one of the rocks facing the sea, a book in his hands, a pair of sunglasses perched insecurely on the bridge of his nose. As she moved forward and began to scramble towards him he caught sight of her and waved.

"Hullo," he said when she was in earshot. "I thought you were resting."

141

"I decided I didn't want to waste such a lovely afternoon." She ignored his outstretched hand and climbed up on to the rock beside him. The tide was still rising and before them the surf thundered among the boulders and reefs in great white clouds of spray.

"I see," said Alexander. His skin was already tanned, she noticed. He had probably been abroad that summer. His chest and shoulders were muscular but were beginning to run to fat. She thought of Jon's body suddenly, remembered the powerful lines and hard flesh and strong muscles, and suddenly she wondered how often Max Alexander had been compared with his friend in the past and how often the comparison had been unfavorable.

"Tell me about yourself," Alexander said sociably, closing the book and fumbling for a cigarette. "How on Earth did you come to be in a god-forsaken country like Canada?"

She started to talk. It was difficult at first, for she was shy, but gradually she began to relax and speech came more easily. He helped her by being relaxed himself.

"I've been mixed up in motor racing most of my adult life," he said casually when she asked him a question about his hobbies. "It's a hell of a thing to get mixed up in. It's all right if you want to play chess with death and have half your face burnt off and get kicks out of a fast car and the smell of scorched rubber, but otherwise it's not much fun. I've more or less had enough."

"What are you going to do now, then?"

"Depends on how long I live," he said laconically. "I have heart trouble. I'll probably go on doing damn all and paying my taxes until I drop dead, I should think."

She wasn't sure how she should reply. Perhaps she was beginning to sense that he wasn't nearly as relaxed and casual as he appeared to be.

"It must be strange for you to come back here," she said suddenly after a pause. "Are you glad you came?"

He swiveled his body slightly to face her, and the sun shone straight into the lenses of his dark glasses so that she could not see his expression.

"It's nice to see Jon again," he said at last. "We'd drifted right apart. I was rather surprised when he rang up and said he wanted to bury the hatchet. . . . There was a hatchet, you know. Or did you?"

"Yes," she said, lying without hesitation. "Jon told me."

"Did he? Yes, I suppose he would have." He fidgeted idly with the corner of his book. "When I knew he was going back to Clougy, I—well, quite frankly I was astonished. So astonished that I couldn't resist coming down here when the opportunity arose to find out why he'd come back." There was a little tear in the dust-jacket of his book, and he tore the paper off at right-angles so that he had a small yellow triangle of paper in his hand. "I didn't know Marijohn was living here."

"Jon was very anxious to see her before he returned to Canada."

"Yes," said Alexander. "I dare say he was."

"Jon told me all about it."

He looked at her sharply again. "About what?"

"About himself and Marijohn."

"I didn't know," said Alexander, "that there was anything to tell."

"Well . . ." She was nonplussed suddenly, at a loss for words. "He said how fond of her he was as they'd spent some of their childhood together."

"Oh, I see." He sat up a little and yawned unconcernedly. "Yes, they're very fond of each other." For a moment she thought he wasn't going to say any more and then without warning he said abruptly: "What do you think of Marijohn?"

"I—"

"Sophia hated her; did Jon tell you that as well? To begin with, of course, it didn't matter because Jon worshipped the ground Sophia walked on and for Sophia the world was her oyster. She could say, do, want anything she wished. A pleasant position for a woman to be in, wouldn't you think? Unfortunately Sophia didn't know how lucky she was—she had to abuse her position until one day she discovered she hadn't any position left and her worshipping husband was a complete stranger to her." He drew on his cigarette for a moment and watched the surf pound upon the rocks a few yards away before being sucked back into the ocean with the roar of the undertow. "But of course—I was forgetting. Jon's told you all about that."

The waves were eating greedily across the shingle again swirling round the rocks.

"I felt sorry for Sophia," said Alexander after a while. "I think I was the only person who did. Marijohn despised her; Jon became totally indifferent to her; Michael—well, God, a conventional pillar of society such as Michael would always look down his nose at a sexy little foreign girl like Sophia who had no more moral sense than a kitten! But I felt sorry for her. It was terrible at the end, you know. She couldn't understand it—she didn't know what to do. I mean, Christ, what was there to do? There was nothing there, you see, nothing at all. It wasn't as if she'd caught Jon in bed with someone else. It wasn't as if he'd thrashed her with a horsewhip twice a day. There was nothing tangible, nothing you could pinpoint, nothing you could grasp and say, 'Look, this is what's wrong! Stop it at once!' She discovered quite suddenly that her loving husband didn't give a damn about her, and she didn't even know how it had happened."

"Maybe she deserved it. If she was constantly unfaithful to Jon—"

"Oh God, it wasn't like that! She behaved like a spoiled child and grumbled and sulked and complained, but she wasn't unfaithful. She flirted at her weekend parties and made Jon go through hell, time and again with her tantrums and whims, but she wasn't unfaithful. What chance did she have to be unfaithful stuck down here at the back of beyond? And anyway underneath her complaints and sulks she probably found Jon attractive enough and it was pleasant to be adored and worshipped all the time. It was only when she realized that she'd lost him that she was unfaithful in an attempt to win him back."

Sarah stared at him.

"And he didn't give a damn. She flaunted her infidelity and he was indifferent. She was sexy as hell in an attempt to seduce him back to her bed and he was still indifferent. It was a terrible thing for a woman like Sophia whose only weapons were her sex and her femininity. When she found both were worthless she had nothing—she'd reached the end of the road. And still he didn't care."

"He—" The words stuck in Sarah's throat. "He must have cared a little. If he'd loved her so much—"

"He didn't give a damn." He threw away his cigarette and the glowing tip hissed as it touched the seaweed pool below. "I'll tell you exactly what happened so that you can see for yourself.

"I came down to Clougy that weekend with a friend called Eve. We were having an affair, as I'm sure Jon

145

has told you, but at that particular stage the affair was wearing rather thin. We arrived on Friday evening, spent an unsatisfactory night together and quarreled violently after breakfast the next morning. Not a very bright start to a long weekend by the sea! After the quarrel she locked herself in her room or something equally dramatic, and I went out to my car with the idea of going for a spin along the coast road to St. Ives or over the hills to Penzance. I find driving soothing after unpleasant scenes.

"I was just getting into the car when Sophia came out. God, I can see her now! She wore skin-tight black slacks and what Americans would call a 'halter'—some kind of flimsy arrangement which left her midriff bare, and exposed an indecent amount of cleavage. Her hair was loose, waving round her face and falling over her shoulders in the style which Brigitte Bardot made so famous. 'Ah Max!' she said, smiling brilliantly, 'are you going into St. Ives? Take me with you!' She made it sound so exactly like an invitation to bed that I just stood and gaped, and then as I started to stammer 'Of course' or something mundane, Jon came out of the front door and called out to her, but she took no notice, merely sliding into the passenger seat and wriggling into a comfortable position.

" 'Sophia', he said again, coming over to the car. 'I want to talk to you.'

"She just shrugged idly and said she was going into St. Ives with me to buy shellfish for dinner that night. Then Jon turned on me. 'Did you invite her,' he said furiously, 'or did she invite herself?'

" 'Jon darling,' said Sophia before I could reply, 'you're making *su-uch* an exhibition of yourself.' She had the habit of drawing out some syllables and thickening her foreign accent sometimes when she was annoyed.

"Jon was shaking with rage. I could only stand and watch him helplessly. 'You're the one who's making an exhibition of yourself!' he shouted at her. 'Do you think I didn't notice how you did your damnedest to flirt with Max last night? Do you think Eve didn't notice? Why do you think she and Max quarreled this morning? I'll not have my wife behaving like a whore whenever we have guests down here. Either you get out of that car and stop acting the part of a prostitute or I'll put a stop to your weekend parties once and for all.'

" 'Look, Jon—' I tried to say, but he wouldn't listen to me. I did my best to pour oil on troubled waters, but I was wasting my breath.

" 'That's ridiculous!' cried Sophia, and she was as furious as hell too. 'Your stupid jealousy! I want to get some shellfish for dinner and Max is going to St. Ives —why shouldn't he give me a lift there? Why shouldn't he?'

"Well, of course, put like that it did make it seem as if Jon was making a fuss about nothing. But there she sat in the front seat of my car, her hair tumbling over her shoulders, her breasts all but spilling out of that scanty halter, her mouth sulky—Christ, any husband would have had the excuse for thinking or suspecting or fearing all kinds of things! 'You'd better stay, Sophia,' I said. 'I'll get your shellfish for you. Tell me what you want.'

" 'No,' she said. 'I'm coming with you.'

"It was extremely embarrassing. I didn't know what to do. She was looking at Jon and he was looking at her, and I was just trying to work out how I could tactfully make my escape when there was the sneeze from the porch. Jon and I swung round. It was the child. He'd been standing listening, I suppose, poor

147

little bastard, and wondering what the hell was going on. After he sneezed, he turned to sidle indoors again but Jon called out to him and he came sheepishly out into the sunlight.

" 'Come on, Justin,' Jon said, taking him by the hand. 'We're going down to the Flat Rocks.'

"He didn't say anything else. He took the child's hand in his and the child looked up at him trustingly, and the next moment they were walking across the lawn away from us and we were alone.

"So we went to St. Ives. It was a hot day, rather like this one, and after we'd bought the shellfish we paused at one of the coves down the coast to bathe. I've forgotten what the cove was called. It was very small and you could only reach it when the tide was out a certain distance. No one else was there.

"I don't make excuses for what happened. I made love with my best friend's wife, and there can be no excuse for that—no valid excuse. Of course it was Sophia who suggested the swim, and Sophia who knew the cove, and Sophia who took off her clothes first and Sophia who made the first physical contact with her hands, but what if it was? I suppose if I'd had half an ounce of decency I could have said no all along the line, but I didn't. I suppose I'm not really a particularly decent person. And there were other reasons . . . Jon had often taken things of mine, you see. I'd had girls and then as soon as they saw Jon they weren't interested in me any more. He was interested in motor-racing for a while, and when I introduced him to the right contacts it turned out that he could drive better than I could and the contacts became more interested in him than in me. Oh, there were other situations too, other memories. . . . It wasn't Jon's fault. It was just the way he was made. But I built up quite a store of resentment all the same, a long list of grudges which I barely acknowledged even to myself. When his wife was mine for the taking, I never even hesitated.

"We arrived back at Clougy at about four o'clock in the afternoon. Everyone was very still. At first we thought everyone must be out, and then we heard the piano.

" 'He's crazy,' said Sophia indolently. 'Imagine playing the piano indoors on a beautiful afternoon like this!' And she walked down the corridor and opened the door of the music room. 'Jon—' she began and then stopped. I walked down to see why she had stopped, and then I saw that Jon wasn't alone in the music room. Marijohn was with him.

"I can't describe how strange it was. There was no reason why it should be strange at all. Marijohn was sitting on the window-seat, very relaxed and happy, and Jon was on the piano-stool, casual and at ease. They weren't even within six feet of each other.

" 'Hullo,' said Marijohn to Sophia, and her eyes were very blue and clear and steady. 'Did you manage to get the shellfish in St. Ives?' I'll always remember the way she said that because I saw then for the first time how much she despised Sophia. 'Did you manage to get the shellfish in St. Ives?'

"And Sophia said, 'Where's Michael?'

"Marijohn said she had no idea. And Jon said, 'Didn't he go fishing?' And they laughed together and Jon started to play again.

"We might as well not have existed.

" 'I'm going down to the cove with Max,' said Sophia suddenly.

" 'Oh yes?' Jon said, turning a page of music with one hand.

" 'Don't get too sunburnt,' said Marijohn. 'The sun's hot today, isn't it, Jon?'

" 'Very,' said Jon, and went on playing without looking up.

"So we went out. Sophia was furious although she said nothing. And then when we arrived at the beach we found the child was following us, and she vented her temper on him, telling him to go away. Poor little bastard! He looked so lost and worried. He wandered off along the shore and was soon lost from sight amongst the rocks.

"We had a swim and after that Sophia started to talk. She talked about Marijohn, and in the end she started to cry. 'I hate it when she comes here,' she said. 'I hate it. Nothing ever goes right when she comes.' And when I asked what Marijohn did, she couldn't explain and only cried all the more. There was nothing, you see, that was what was so baffling. There was nothing there to explain. . . .

"I was just trying to console her and take her in my arms when the worst thing possible happened—Eve had heard I was back from St. Ives and had come down from her room to look for me. Of course she found me in what I believe is generally termed a 'compromising' position, so there was another row and she went back to the house. She didn't come down to dinner that evening.

"Dinner was very unnerving. Sophia had been supervising the cooking in the kitchen so we didn't come into the diningroom together, but it was obvious she had decided to act the part of the good hostess and be bright and talkative, pretending nothing had happened at all. I responded as best as I could and Michael joined in from time to time, I remember. But

Marijohn and Jon never said a word. Gradually, after a while, their silence became oppressive. It's very difficult to describe. One was so conscious somehow of their joint silence. If one had been silent and the other talkative it wouldn't have mattered, but it was their joint silence which was so uncanny. In the end Sophia fell silent too, and I could think of nothing more to say, and Michael was quiet. And it was then, when the whole room was silent, that Marijohn started to speak.

"She talked exclusively to Jon. They discussed music, I remember, a topic which was open to no one but themselves because no one else knew much about it. They talked to one another for ten minutes, and then suddenly they were silent again and I was so taut with uneasiness I could scarcely move my knife and fork. Presently Sophia told the child to go to bed. He made rather a fuss, I remember, and didn't want to go, but in the end Michael took him upstairs. I remember having the strong impression that Michael wanted to escape. . . . We all stood up from the table then and Jon went out into the hall. He put on a red sweater and Sophia said: 'You're not going out, are you?' and he said, 'Marijohn and I are going for a stroll down to the cove.'

"So they went out. They weren't gone too long, only ten minutes or so and then they came back and went to the music room. Presently Michael came downstairs and went into the music room to join them. I was in the kitchen with Sophia helping her wash up, but when they came back she went to the door to listen. The gramophone was playing. She said, 'I'm going in to see what's happening,' and I said, 'Leave them alone—come out with me for a while. Michael's with them anyway.' And she said, 'Yes, I want to hear what he says.' I told her there was no reason why he should say anything at all, but she said she still wanted to see what was happening.

"We were in the hall by then. She said she would meet me later in the evening—'somewhere where we can be alone,' she said, 'somewhere where we can talk and not be overheard. I'll meet you down by the Flat Rocks at ten o'clock.' When I agreed, she went into the music room and I was alone in the hall. I can remember the scene so clearly. The gramophone stopped a moment later. There was no light in the hall, just the dusk from the twilight outside, and Jon's discarded red sweater lay across the oak chest by the door like a pool of blood.

"I went out soon after that. I walked down to the cove and watched the sea for a while, and then I walked back to the house to get a sweater as it was rather colder than I'd anticipated. After that I went out again, taking the cliff path which led out to the Flat Rocks, and about quarter of an hour later I was waiting by the water's edge."

He stopped. The tide roared over the shingle.

"I waited some time," he said, "but of course Sophia never came. I heard the scream just as I was wondering what could have happened to her, but although I moved as fast as I could she was dead when I reached her."

He stopped again. Presently he took off his sunglasses and she saw the expression in his eyes for the first time.

"Poor Sophia," he said slowly; "it was a terrible thing to happen. I always felt so sorry for Sophia. . . ."

Four

I

JUSTIN WAS in St. Ives by the time the church clock near the harbor was tolling three that afternoon. Holiday-makers thronged the streets, spilling over the pavements to make driving hazardous. The pedestrians ruled St. Ives, dictating to the cars that crawled through the narrow streets, and Justin was relieved when he reached the freedom of the car park at last and was able to switch off the engine. He got out of the car. The air was salt and fresh, the sun deliciously warm. As he walked up the steps along by the town wall the gulls wheeled around the fishing boats in the harbor and the houses clustered on the rising ground of the peninsula were white-walled and strangely foreign beneath that hot southern sky.

Justin reached the harbor, turned up Fish Street and then turned again. There was an alley consisting of stone steps leading to a higher level, and at the top was another narrow cobbled lane slanting uphill. The door marked Five was pale blue. and a climbing plant trailed from the corner of the windows to meet above the porch.

He rang the bell.

A woman answered the door. She had a London accent and London clothes and a paint smear across the back of her left hand.

"Is Eve in?" said Justin hesitantly, suddenly nervous.

"Ah yes, you're expected, aren't you? Come on in. She's upstairs—second door on the right."

"Thank you." The hall was a mass of brass and copper ornaments. His hand gripped the hand rail of the stairs tightly and then he was walking quietly up the steps, neither pausing nor looking back. The woman was watching him. He could feel her eyes looking him up and down, wondering who he was and what connection he could possibly have with the woman waiting upstairs, but he didn't stop and the next moment he was on the landing and pausing to regain his breath. It suddenly seemed very hot.

The second door on the right was facing him. Presently he took a pace forward and raised his hand to knock.

"Come in," called the woman's voice from beyond as his knuckles touched the wood, and suddenly he was back in the past again, a little boy catching sight of the untasted supper tray outside the closed door and knocking on the panels to inquire if he could eat the food which she had ignored.

He stood rigid, not moving, the memories taut in his mind.

"Come in!" called the woman again, and even as he moved to turn the handle on the door she was opening the door for him so that a second later they were facing each other across the threshold.

No hint of recognition showed in her face. He caught a glimpse of disappointment, then of irritation, and he felt his ears burn scarlet in a sudden rush of embarassment.

"You must want one of the other lodgers," he heard her say shortly. "Who are you looking for?"

He swallowed, all his careful words of introduction forgotten, and wondered vaguely in the midst of all his panic how on Earth he had had the nerve to come. He stared down at her toes. She wore white sandals, cool and elegant, and in spite of his confusion he was aware of thinking that her smart, casual clothes were much too chic and well-tailored for that little holiday resort far from London.

"Wait a minute," she said. "I know you."

He cleared his throat. Presently he had enough confidence to glance up into her eyes. She looked bewildered but not hostile, and he began to feel better.

"You're Justin," she said suddenly.

He nodded.

For a moment she made no move, and then she was opening the door wider and turning back into the room.

"You'd better come in," she said over her shoulder.

He followed her. The room beyond was small with a view from the window of rooftops and a distant glimpse of the sun sparkling on blue sea.

"You're not much like either of your parents, are you?" she said absently, sitting down on the stool of the crowded dressing-table and flicking ash into a souvenir ashtray. "I hardly recognized you. You've lost such a lot of weight."

He smiled warily, easing himself on to the edge of the bed.

"Well," she said at last when the silence threatened to become prolonged. "Why have you come? Have you got a message from your father?"

"No," he said, "he doesn't know you're here. Your note reached me by mistake and I didn't show it to him. I didn't see why you should bother my father when he's still more or less on his honeymoon."

She was annoyed. As she swiveled round to face him, he could see the anger in her eyes. "Just what the hell do you think you're playing at?" she demanded coldly.

He had forgotten his panic and shyness now. He

stared back at her defiantly. "You wanted to talk about what happened at Clougy ten years ago," he said. "You wanted to talk about Max."

"To your father. Not to you."

"I know more than you think I do."

She smiled, looking skeptical. "How can you?" she said. "You were just a child at the time. You couldn't have understood what was happening so how can you know anything about it?"

"Because I saw my mother's death," he said, and even as he spoke he saw her eyes widen and her expression change. "I saw it all, don't you see? I followed the murderer up on the cliffs that night and saw him push my mother down the cliff-path to her death. . . ."

II

Sarah left the beach soon after five and walked up to the house to see if Jon had returned from his visit to Penzance. Alexander stayed behind in the cove. When she reached the drive she saw that a blue Hillman was parked behind Max's silver-gray Rolls Royce and she wondered who the visitors were and whether they had been there long.

The hall was cool and shadowed after the shimmering brilliance of the early evening, and she paused for a moment before the mirror to adjust her hair before crossing the hall and opening the drawing-room door.

Marijohn was sitting at the desk by the window. There was a pen in her hand. Behind her, slightly to her left so that he could look over her shoulder was a tall man, unobtrusively good-looking, with quiet eyes and a strong mouth. Both he and Marijohn looked up with a start as Sarah came into the room.

"Oh, it's only you." Marijohn put down the pen for a moment. "Michael dear, this is Sarah. . . . Sarah —Michael Rivers."

"How do you do," said Rivers, giving her a pleasant smile while looking at her with lawyer's eyes. And then as she echoed the greeting, the lawyer's cautious scrutiny faded into a more formal appraisal and there was warmth in his eyes and kindness in the set of his mouth. "May I offer my congratulations on your marriage? I expect belated congratulations are better than none at all."

"Thank you," she said shyly. "Thank you very much."

There was a pause. She said awkwardly, as if to explain her presence, "I—I just wondered if Jon was back yet? He didn't say what time he would be returning from Penzance, but I thought perhaps—"

"No," said Marijohn, "he's not here yet." She turned to Michael. "Darling, how many more of these do I have to sign?"

"Just the transfer here . . ." He bent over her again and something in the way he moved made Sarah stop to watch them. Phrases of Justin's sprang back to her mind. "It was obvious he loved her. He kissed her in public and gave her special smiles—oh God, you know! The sort of thing you notice and squirm at when you're a small boy. . . ."

It seemed strange to know they were divorced.

"Fine," said Rivers, gathering up the papers as Marijohn put down her pen. "I'll take these back with me to London tomorrow."

"Are you staying near here?"

"With the Hawkins over at Mullion."

"The Hawkins! Of course! Do they still live in that funny little cottage by the harbor?"

"No, they—" He stopped, listening.

157

Marijohn was listening, too.

Sarah felt her heart begin to thump faster as she too turned to face the door.

From far away came the sound of footsteps crunching on the gravel of the drive.

"That'll be Jon," said Rivers. "Well, I must be going. I'll phone you about the outcome of those transfers and contact Mathieson in the city about the gilt-edged question."

But Marijohn was still listening. The footsteps echoed in the porch and then moved through the open front door into the hall.

There was an inexplicable pause—the footsteps halted.

"Jon!" called Marijohn suddenly.

The latch clicked; the door swung wide.

"Hullo," said Jon, unsurprised and unperturbed. "How are you, Michael? Hullo, Sarah darling—feeling better now?" And as the others watched he stooped to give her a kiss.

"Much better," she said, clasping his hand tightly as he kissed her and releasing it only when he moved away towards the desk.

Jon turned to Rivers. "Why didn't you ring up to tell us you were coming, Michael? Are you staying to dinner?"

"No," said Rivers. "I'm spending a couple of days with friends at Mullion, and just called in to discuss one or two business matters with Marijohn."

"Phone your friends and say you're dining out tonight. They wouldn't mind, would they? Stay and have dinner with us!"

"I'm afraid that's not possible," said Rivers pleasantly. "But thank you all the same."

"Marijohn!" said Jon to his cousin, his eyes bright, his frame taut and vibrant with life. "You'd like Michael

158

to stay for dinner, wouldn't you? Persuade him to stay!"

Marijohn's eyes were very clear. She turned to Rivers. "Won't you, Michael?" was all she said. "Please."

He shrugged, making a helpless gesture with his hands, and then she gave him a warm, brilliant, unexpected smile and he was lost. "When did you last have dinner with me?"

He shrugged again, not replying, but Sarah saw him bend his head slowly in acquiescence and knew that he had agreed to stay against his better judgment.

"Where's Max, Sarah?" said Jon to her, making her jump.

"He—he's still down by the cove, sunbathing."

"And Justin?"

"Still in St. Ives presumably," said Marijohn, moving over to the French windows. "Michael, come out and sit on the swing-seat and forget all those dreary legal documents for a while. I expect Jon wants to be alone with Sarah."

That was said for effect, thought Sarah instantly and unreasonably. All this is for effect to make some definite impression on Michael. This is all for Michael. And Jon is playing the same game; he's set the key for the evening and she's responding note for note. The key involved inviting Michael to dinner, giving the impression that the past is buried and forgotten, and now they want to show him that everything is normal and that there's nothing to hide.

Her thoughts raced on and on, no matter how hard she tried to stem her rising feeling of panic. How could Jon and Marijohn be working in conjunction with one another when Jon hadn't even known Michael was calling in that evening? But he had known. He had walked into the room and said "Hullo, Michael" although he could not have known before he opened the door that

Michael would be there. . . . Perhaps he had recognized Michael's car. But the car wasn't ten years old! Jon could never have seen the car before. And yet he had known, he had known before he had opened the door that he would find Michael with Marijohn in the room . . .

"Come upstairs and talk to me, darling," said Jon, putting his arm round her waist. "I want to shower and change my clothes. Come and tell me what you've been doing."

So she went upstairs and sat on the edge of the bath as he had a shower and then rubbed himself vigorously with the rough towel. He told her about his friend in Penzance and described the motor-boat and the afternoon spin on the sea in detail. Finally as he returned to the bedroom to dress he paused to smile at her.

"Now tell me what you've been doing! You've hardly said a word to me all day! Do you still love me?"

There was a lump in her throat suddenly, a deep unreasoning ache that only deepened against her will. "Oh Jon," was all she could say, and then the next moment she was in his arms and pressing her face against his chest and he was crushing the sobs from her body and kissing her eyes to stop her tears.

"Sarah," he said, upset. "Sarah, darling Sarah, what is it? What's the matter? What have I said?"

"I—" She summoned together all her strength and managed to look straight into his eyes. "Jon," she said. "Jon, I want something very badly. Could you—"

"Tell me what it is," he said instantly, "and you shall have it. Just tell me what it is."

She took a deep breath, checked her tears. "I—I want to go back to Canada, Jon—I don't want to stay here. I just want to go home. Please, Jon, let's go. I don't want to stay here. I'm terribly sorry, but I—"

"I don't understand," he said. "Why don't you want to stay? I was planning to stay for another week."

She couldn't cry now. She could only stare into his face and think: It's all true. There *is* something. Max wasn't lying. There's something intangible, something impossible to describe, just as he said there was. It's all true.

"I thought you liked it here," he said. "What's wrong? What is it?"

She shook her head dumbly. "Marijohn—"

"What about Marijohn?" he said. He spoke much too quickly, and afterwards looked annoyed with himself for betraying his feelings.

"She doesn't like me."

"Rubbish. She thinks you're very pretty and just right for me and she's very glad I've married someone so nice."

She twisted away from him, but he held her tightly and wouldn't let her go. "Come here."

The towel slipped from his waist. He pulled her down on the bed and suddenly she clung to him in a rush of passion and desire which was terrible to her because she was so afraid it would strike no response in him.

"Sarah . . ." He sounded surprised, taken aback but not indifferent. And suddenly his passion was flowing into her own, and the more she poured out her love to him in movement and gesture the more he took her love and transformed it with his own.

When they parted at last the sweat was blinding her eyes and there were tears on her cheeks and her body felt bruised and aching.

"I love you," she said. "I love you."

He was still trying to find his breath, still trembling, his fists clenched with his tension and his eyes tight shut for a second as if in pain. He can't relax, she

161

thought, and neither can I. There's no peace. We should be able to sleep now for a while but we won't. There's no peace here, no rest.

"Jon," she said. "Jon darling, take me away from here. Let's go tomorrow. Please. Let's go back to London, back to Canada, anywhere, but don't let's stay here anymore."

His fists were clenched so tightly that the skin was white across the knuckles. "Why?" he said indistinctly into the pillow, his voice truculent and hostile. "Why? Give me one good reason."

And when she was silent he reached out and pulled her towards him in a violent gesture of love. "Give me another couple of days," he said. "Please. If you love me, give me that. I can't go just yet."

She tried to frame the word "why" but it refused to come. She got up, went into the bathroom and washed, but when she returned from the bathroom she found that he was still lying in the same position. She started to dress.

Time passed.

At last, sitting down in front of the mirror, she began to do her hair but still she made no attempt to speak, and the silence between them remained unbroken.

"Sarah," Jon said at last in distress. "Sarah, please."

She swiveled round to face him. "Is Marijohn your mistress?"

There was utter silence. He stared at her, his eyes dark and opaque.

"No," he said at last. "Of course not. Sarah—"

"Has she ever been your mistress?"

"No!" he said with sudden violent resentment. "Never!"

"Were you having an affair with her when Sophia was killed?"

"No!" he shouted, springing off the bed and coming across the room towards her. "No, no, no!" He took her by the shoulders and started to shake her. "No, no, no—"

"Jon," she said gently. "Shhh, Jon . . ."

He sank down beside her on the stool. "If that's why you want to leave, you can forget it," he said tightly. "There's nothing like that between us. She—" He stopped.

"She?"

"She detests any form of physical love," he said. "Didn't you guess? She can't even bear being touched however casually by a man. Did you never notice how I've always avoided touching her? Did you never notice how I didn't kiss her when we met? Didn't you notice any of those things?"

She stared at him. He stared back, his hands trembling.

"I see," she said, at last.

He relaxed, and she knew in a flash that he had not understood. He thought she understood only the key to Marijohn's remoteness, and he never knew that all she understood was the despair in his eyes and the physical frustration in every line of his tense, taut frame.

III

When Sarah went downstairs the hall was dim and quiet and she decided the others must still be in the garden. There was no sign of Max Alexander. After pausing by the open front door to glance up the hillside and listen to the rushing water beyond the gateway she crossed the hall and opened the drawing-room door.

She had been wrong. Rivers and Marijohn were no longer in the garden. As she entered the room, Rivers

163

swung round abruptly to face the door and Marijohn glanced up from her position on the sofa.

"I—I'm sorry," stammered Sarah. "I thought—"

"That's all right," Rivers said easily, lulling her feeling of embarrassment. "Come on in. We were just wondering whether Max has been washed away by the tide down in the cove."

Marijohn stood up. She wore a plain linen dress, narrow and simple, without sleeves. It was a beautiful color. She wore no makeup and no jewelry, and Sarah noticed for the first time that she had even removed her wedding-ring.

"Where are you going?" said Rivers sharply.

"Just to see about dinner." She moved over to the door, not hurrying, her eyes not watching either of them, and went out into the hall.

There was a silence.

"Drink, Sarah?" said Rivers at last.

"No, thank you." She sat down, twisting the material of her dress into tight ridges across her thighs and wondering what Rivers had been saying before she had interrupted him. She was just trying to think of some remark which might begin a polite conversation and ease the silence in the room when Rivers said, "Is Jon upstairs?"

"Yes—yes, he is."

"I see." He was by the sideboard, his hand on the decanter. "Sure you won't join me in a drink?"

She shook her head again and watched him as he mixed himself a whisky and soda.

"How long," he said presently, "are you staying here?"

"I don't know."

He turned to face her abruptly and as she looked at him she saw that he knew.

"You want to go, don't you?"

164

"No," she said, lying out of pride. "No, I like it here."

"I shouldn't stay here too long if I were you."

She shrugged, assuming indifference. "Jon wants to stay here for a day or two longer."

"I'm sure he does." He took a gulp of his drink and she saw his fingers tighten on the stem of his glass. "I didn't realize you would both be coming down here," he said evenly at last. "I didn't think he would be seeing Marijohn again. She had made up her mind not to see him again, I know. I suppose he persuaded her to change her mind."

She stared at him blankly. From somewhere far away she heard the clatter of a saucepan in the kitchen.

"He wanted to see her again—I know that because he came to me in an attempt to find out where she was. Naturally I didn't tell him. I knew she had made up her mind that it would be much better for her not to see him again, and I knew too that it would be disastrous if—"

He stopped.

There were footsteps on the stairs, Jon whistling the old American country song *You Win Again*.

"Listen," said Rivers suddenly. "I must talk to you further about this. It's in both our interests, don't you understand? I must talk to you."

"But I don't see. Why should—"

"You have to get Jon away from here. I can't persuade Marijohn to leave—we're not even married any more. But you can persuade Jon. God, you're all but on your honeymoon, aren't you? Get him away from here, right away. Back to Canada, anywhere—but get him away from this place."

"From this place?"

"From Marijohn."

The whistling stopped; the door opened.

"Sarah? Ah, there you are! Come on down to the cove with me and rescue Max!"

"I think," said Rivers, "that he's just walking up to the gateway."

"Well, so he is!" Jon moved out on to the lawn. "Max!" he shouted his hand raised in welcome. "Where've you been, you bastard? We thought you'd drowned yourself!"

Rivers was already beside her even as she stood up to follow Jon out on to the lawn.

"Come for a walk with me after supper and I'll explain."

"I—"

"You must," he interrupted. "I don't think you understand the danger you're in."

She felt the color drain from her face as she stared into his eyes. And then Jon was blazing across the silence, bursting back into the room to mix a round of drinks, and Alexander was crossing the threshold of the French windows with a lazy, indolent smile on his face.

"Why, Michael! Fancy that! Just like old times! How are you these days? Still soliciting?"

There was brittle, empty conversation for a few minutes. Max started to expound the virtues of his latest car. Jon, moving across to Sarah, kissed her on the mouth with his back to the others and sat down beside her on the sofa.

"All right?"

When she nodded he put his hand over hers and kept it there. She stared blindly down at his fingers, not hearing Max Alexander's voice, aware of nothing except that Jon was a stranger to her whom she could not trust. It occurred to her dully to wonder if she had ever imagined unhappiness to be like this; it's not the raw nagging edge of desolation, she thought, but the tight darkness of fear. The pain is convex and opaque and absolute.

Marijohn returned to the room fifteen minutes later.

"I suppose Justin's coming back for dinner, Jon?"

He shrugged. "I've no idea. I imagine so."

"Can I get you a drink, Marijohn?"

"No . . . no thanks. I think I'll go out for a while. Dinner will be in about another half hour."

On the sofa Sarah felt Jon stir restlessly.

"Another drink, Jon?" offered Max Alexander from the sideboard.

Jon didn't answer.

"Jon," said Sarah, pressing against him instinctively. "Jon."

"Do you want to come, Michael?" said Marijohn. "I don't want to walk far, just down to the cove and back."

"No," said Rivers. "I'm in the middle of a perfectly good whisky and soda and I want to finish it and have another one to follow."

"Don't look at me, Marijohn," advised Max Alexander. "I've staggered down to the cove and back already this afternoon. I've had my share of exercise today."

Jon stood up, hesitated and then reached for the cigarette box to help himself to a cigarette.

"Do you want to go, Jon?" said Rivers pleasantly.

"Not particularly." He lit the cigarette, wandered over to the fireplace and started to straighten the ornaments on the mantelshelf.

Marijohn walked away across the lawn. She walked very slowly, as if savoring each step. Jon glanced after her once and then abruptly turned his back on the window and flung himself down in the nearest armchair.

"Why don't you go, Jon?" said Rivers. "Don't feel you have to stay here and entertain us—I'm sure Sarah would make an admirable hostess. Why don't you go with Marijohn?"

Jon inhaled from his cigarette and watched the blue smoke curl upwards from between his fingers. "We've been down to the sea already today."

"Oh, I see. . . . Not to the Flat Rocks, by any chance?"

"I say," said Alexander suddenly, "what the hell's Justin doing in St.—"

"No," said Jon to Rivers. "Just down to the cove."

"How strange. Marijohn told me she hadn't been down to the cove today."

"Sarah," said Max. "Do you know what Justin's doing in St. Ives?"

"Do you often come down here?" said Jon idly to Rivers. "It must take up a lot of your time if you have to visit Marijohn personally whenever it's necessary to discuss some business problem with her. Or do you like to have a good excuse to visit her as often as possible?"

"At least," said Rivers, "my excuse for coming here is a damned sight better than yours."

"Look," said Max, spilling his drink slightly on the carpet, "for Christ's sake, why doesn't one of you go down to the cove with Marijohn now? Michael, she asked you—why the hell don't you go if you've come down here to see her?"

Jon flung his cigarette into the fireplace and stood up. "Come on, Sarah, we'll go down together."

There was a silence. They were all looking at her.

"No," she said too loudly, "no, I don't want to come. I'd rather stay here."

Jon shrugged his shoulders. "Just as you like," he said

168

shortly, sounding as if he couldn't have cared less, and walked through the open French windows across the lawn without even a hint of a backward glance.

IV

In St. Ives the white houses were basking in the golden glow of evening and the sea was still and calm. In the little house in one of the back-alleys near Fish Street, Justin was holding a mug of steaming coffee in his hands and wondering what had possessed him to tell this woman the story of his life. It was her fault. If she had not questioned him so closely about the aftermath of that terrible weekend at Clougy he would not have needed to explain anything about his grandmother and the parting from his father, but for some reason he had wanted to explain. At first he had been guarded and cautious, but when she had seemed to understand he had lost some of his reserve. She hadn't laughed at him. As the afternoon slid gently away from them, he began to trust her sufficiently to be able to talk more freely.

"And you never told anyone what you saw that night?" she said at last. "You said nothing?"

"I didn't think it would help my father."

"But you're sure now that he didn't kill her."

"He told me he didn't. Someone else must have killed her. I have to find out who it was."

She thought about it for a long moment, and the smoke from her cigarette curled lazily upwards until it was caught in the slanting rays of sunlight and transformed into a golden haze.

"I thought at the time that Jon had probably killed her," she said at last. "But it was a mere suspicion backed up by the knowledge that he had more than enough provocation that weekend. . . . And then last week Max phoned me and asked me out to dinner. As soon as I saw him I realized he was itching to discuss his meeting with Jon earlier and speculate on why Jon should return to Clougy. We talked for hours, recalling all our memories, and in the end he said Jon had half-invited him down to Clougy and he had a good mind to accept in order to have the chance of finding out what was going on. He was convinced that Jon had killed Sophia and he thought it curious, to say the least, that Jon should take his new wife back there ten years later. I'd planned to take a few days' holiday anyway at around this time, and I suddenly thought it might be rather interesting to come down here so that I would be close at hand if Max should discover anything. . . . But the more I thought about Jon and his connection with Sophia's death, the more I felt—" She stopped.

"Felt?"

"I—I felt that it was better to let sleeping dogs lie. . . . After all, it was ten years ago, and Jon's married again now. I suddenly disliked the thought of Max deliberately going down to Clougy with the idea of probing a past which was better buried and forgotten."

"So you wrote to my father to warn him."

"Yes, I thought he should know Max's motives in returning to Clougy." She leant forward and stubbed out her cigarette. "Odd how convinced Max was that she had been murdered. . . . After all, murder was never mentioned at the time, was it? And the jury at the inquest decided it was an accident. But maybe we all knew she'd been murdered although we were too frightened to say so. That's ironic, isn't it! We all had a motive, you see, each one of us. We all had a reason for killing her, so we all kept silent and accepted the verdict of accident because we were afraid of casting suspicion on ourselves by speaking our suspicions aloud to the police. . . . What's the matter? Didn't you guess I might have had a motive for wishing your mother dead?"

He shook his head wordlessly, watching her.

"I was an outsider from the first," she said, lighting another cigarette and shaking out the match as she spoke. "They all belonged to a different world—all of them except Sophia, and even her world of Soho cafés wasn't exactly mine. I was only eighteen then; I hadn't been working in London for very long. I met Max by accident at some party which I and a few friends had gate-crashed and I didn't know the kind of man he was. I just knew he was rich and moved in an expensive, exciting world, and I didn't find it difficult to fall in love and start to imagine all kinds of exotic, romantic pictures. It's so easy when one's only eighteen to live with one's head in the clouds, isn't it? Anyway, we had an affair, and eventually he took me to Clougy for that weekend.

"I was still in love with him then, still dreaming my romantic little daydreams.

"I think I hated Clougy from the first moment that I saw it. As for the other people, I didn't understand them at all—God, how baffling they seemed at the time! I found Jon interesting but he scarcely seemed to notice I existed—he was entirely engrossed with his wife and his cousin, and cared for nothing else. As for his cousin—well, I had nothing to say to her; we simply didn't even begin to talk the same language. The solicitor-husband was nice but too polite to be friendly, and anyway he too seemed to be almost entirely wrapped up in his personal problems. I disliked Sophia straight away, but it wasn't a very active dislike. I remember thinking that she just seemed rather common and vulgar.

"She started to flirt with Max about an hour after we'd arrived. I didn't take her seriously at first because I thought she surely couldn't flirt with one of her guests under her husband's nose, but that was my mistake. She meant it all right. The next morning Max and I quarreled violently and he went off with Sophia to St. Ives on a—quote 'shopping expedition,' unquote. I don't think I've ever been so unhappy either before or since. I stayed in my room all morning and until the early evening when I heard them come back from St. Ives. After a while I went to look for Max and you told me—do you remember?—that he'd gone down to the cove with your mother for a swim. So I went out, taking the path down to the beach.

"I heard them talking before I saw them. She was saying in that ugly foreign voice of hers that she had a wonderful scheme all planned. She was sick to death of Clougy and wanted to get away from Jon and go back to London, and Max was to be her savior. She had it all worked out—a cosy little ménage à deux with just the right-sized luxury flat in Mayfair and maybe a cosy little divorce at the end of the rainbow. It sounded wonderful. God, how I hated her! I can't describe how much I hated her at that moment. And then I realized that Max wasn't exactly enthralled with all these beautiful schemes and I suddenly wanted to laugh out loud. He tried to put it tactfully at first but when she refused to understand, he spoke more frankly. He didn't want a ménage à deux in Mayfair or the scandal and publicity of being correspondent in his best friend's divorce suit! The last thing he wanted was to have Sophia permanently on his hands in London! He didn't really want an affair with the woman at all and the

172

thought of her shouting from the rooftops that she was his mistress was enough to make his blood run cold. 'Look,' he said to her. 'I can't and won't play your game the way you want it played. You'd better find yourself another lover.' And then just as I was closing my eyes in sheer relief I heard the woman say, 'I have to get away from here—you don't understand. I'll go mad if I have to stay here any longer. If you don't take me to London and give me money and somewhere to live I'll make you the most famous correspondent in town and blow your friendship with Jon to smithereens.'

"And Max said with a laugh, 'You wouldn't have a hope in heaven of doing either of those things!'

" 'Wouldn't I?' she said. 'Wouldn't I? Just you try and see!'

"And after a moment Max said, 'I'd better have time to think about this and then I'll have to talk to you again. I'll meet you out at the Flat Rocks after dinner this evening and we can discuss the situation in detail.'

"I moved then. I came round the rocks towards them and Max saw straight away that I'd heard what they'd been saying. When he lost his temper with me and asked me what the hell I thought I was doing spying on him, I turned on Sophia and called her all the names I could think of. I blamed her for everything—Max's changed attitude towards me, my own misery, his violent loss of temper which upset me more than anything else in the world. And she just laughed. I stormed and raged and poured out abuse and all she did was laugh.

"I found my way back to the house somehow. I went to my room and stayed there while I shed enough tears to fill the Atlantic Ocean. I knew then that everything was finished as far as Max and I were concerned, and that I meant no more to him than Sophia—or any other woman—did. I'd been deceiving myself for weeks that he cared for me, and I knew then that I'd been both incredibly blind and incredibly stupid. But I was only eighteen . . . It's so easy to make mistakes at eighteen, isn't it?"

"I knew what time he was going to meet Sophia. I thought that if I could see him for a few minutes alone, if I could meet him by the Flat Rocks before Sophia arrived, I could perhaps persuade him not to listen to her, to call her bluff, and perhaps I could show him how much I still loved him. But I didn't know where the Flat Rocks were or how one reached them. In the end on an impulse I went out of my room and moved downstairs. It was late. There was a hell of a row going on in the music room, but I didn't stop to listen. I went outside to the gate to see if there was any sign of Max leaving for the Flat Rocks, and just as I reached the gate I saw him; he was walking down towards the beach. At the head of the cove he paused to watch the sea for a few minutes, and then he turned to retrace his steps and he saw me straight away. When I asked him where he was going he shrugged and said he was going back to the house.

" 'I thought you'd gone to keep your rendezvous with Sophia,' I said. 'Why have you come back?'

" 'It's colder than I thought,' he said. 'I've come back for a sweater.'

"I tried to talk with him then, pleading with him to ignore Sophia and begging him to take me back to London straight away, but it was no good. He wouldn't listen, and just told me not to try to organize his life for him as he was perfectly capable of organizing it himself. When we reached the house again, he left me while he went inside to fetch his sweater, and I waited

174

in the bushes by the gate, meaning to follow him when he came out again.

"He came out again almost at once.

"I followed him a little way, but he must have seen me for he lay in wait and stepped out in front of me as I reached the point where the path forked to go up to the cliffs. We had one final bitter useless row there and then he went on out towards the Flat Rocks while I sat down on a rock near the fork in the path and tried to pull myself together.

"When I finally went back to the house there was a light on in the music room where I had heard them all quarreling earlier, but the door was open now and no one was there. I was just standing in the hall and wondering where they all were when Jon came down the stairs. 'Marijohn' he called, seeing my shadow on the wall and thinking I was his cousin, and then he saw it was me. 'Where's Marijohn?' he said. 'Where's she gone?' I shook my head. He was very white. 'I have to find her. I have to find Marijohn.' He kept saying it over and over again. 'Where is everyone?' he said at last. 'Where's Max?' I told him then, and he went straight away to the front door, stopping for a moment by the chest as if he were pausing to look for something, but there was nothing there. The next moment he was in the drive and I was alone again in the hall."

She shook ashes from her cigarette onto the carpet. "I didn't kill your mother," she said at last. "I could have done it, but I didn't. I went up to my room again and stayed there until Max came up to tell me the news."

There was a silence in the room. When she next glanced at him she saw to her surprise that he was leaning forward and his eyes were dark with concentration.

"My father was at the house when you returned to it from the cove?"

"Why, yes," she said. "I told you."

"What was he wearing?"

"What was he wearing? God, I haven't the faintest idea! I wasn't in a mood for noticing clothes that night. Why?"

"Was he wearing a red sweater?"

"I don't think so—no, I'm sure he wasn't. When I saw him he was wearing only a shirt and a pair of trousers—I remember noticing that his shirt was open at the neck and I could see the sweat glistening on the skin at his throat. God, he did look shaken! He was white as a sheet and all he could do was ask for Marijohn. . . ."

Five

I

As SOON AS it was dark that evening Sarah made an excuse to go up to her room, and then slipped outside into the cool night air to wait in the shadows by the gate. She didn't have to wait long. As she plucked a leaf from the rhododendron bush nearby and tore it to shreds in her fingers she saw the front door open noiselessly and the next moment Rivers was crossing the drive towards her.

"Sarah?"

"Yes," she said. "I'm here."

"Good." He drew closer to her and she was conscious

of his air of authority. He could cope with the situation, she thought with a rush of relief. He's spent his life dealing with other people's problems and her own problem was something which probably he alone was fully able to understand. "The first thing to do," he said, "is to walk away from the house. I don't want to run the risk of anyone overhearing our conversation."

"Shall we go down to the cove?"

"No," he said, "that would be the first place they'd look for us. We'll go up on to the cliffs."

They set off along the path, Rivers leading the way, and the night was dark and clouded, muffling the roar of the sea.

"Don't let's go too far," said Sarah suddenly.

"We'll stop around the next corner."

It was much too dark. Sarah found her feet catching in the heather and jarring on the uneven ground.

"Michael—"

"All right," he said. "We'll stop here."

There was an outcrop of rocks below the path and he helped her down the hillside until they could sit side by side on a rocky ledge and watch the dark mass of the sea straight in front of them. Far below them the surf was a fleck of whiteness on the reefs and lagoons of the shore.

"Cigarette?" said Rivers.

"No, thank you."

"Mind if I do?"

"No, not at all." How polite we are, she thought. We should be in a stately London drawing-room instead of on Cornish cliffs at night far from the formalities of civilization.

"How did you meet Jon?" he said suddenly, jolting her away from her thoughts.

She tried to concentrate on the effort of conversation.

"We met through a friend of mine," she said. "Frank's business was connected with Jon's, and one night we all had dinner together—Frank and I, Jon and some girl whom I didn't know. It never occurred to me at the time that Jon was the slightest bit interested in me, but the next day he phoned and asked to take me out to a concert. I went. I shouldn't have because of Frank, but then . . . well, Frank and I weren't engaged, and I—I wanted to see Jon again."

"I see." The cigarette tip glowed red in the darkness and flickered as he inhaled. "Yes, that sounds like Jon."

She said nothing, waiting for him to go on, and, after a moment, he said, "I met both Jon and Marijohn when old Towers died. I was then the assistant solicitor in the firm which had looked after his legal affairs and I was helping the senior partner in the task of proving the will and winding up the estate. Marijohn was eighteen. I'll never forget when I first saw her."

The cigarette tip glowed again.

"I managed to take her out once or twice, but there were about ten other men all wanting to take her out and there are only seven evenings in a week. They had more money and were older and more sophisticated than I was. She always chose the older men; the ones that mattered were all over thirty-five, but I was still fool enough to go on trying and hoping . . . until I went to the party and heard people talking about her. It was then for the first time that I realized she was completely and utterly promiscuous and slept with any man who would give her the best time.

"I left her alone for a while after that, but then I met her again and it was impossible to put her out of my mind. I had to keep phoning her, finding out who she was living with, going through a self-induced hell every day and night. And it was all for nothing, of course. She didn't give a damn.

"Then, quite suddenly, everything changed. One of her affairs went very, very wrong and she had to have an abortion. She had no money and was very ill. And she came to me. It was I who helped her, I who put up the money, arranged the abortion, paid off the necessary doctors—I, a solicitor, committing a criminal offense! But nobody ever found out. Gradually she got better and I took her away to a quiet corner in Sussex for a while to convalesce, but she wasn't fit enough to sleep with me even if she'd wanted to, and after a week she left me and went back to London.

"I followed her back and found she was planning to go down to Cornwall. 'I want to see Jon,' she said to me. I can see her now, standing there, her eyes very blue and clear. She was wearing a dark blue dress which was too big for her because she'd lost so much weight. 'I don't want you to come,' she said. 'I want to be alone with Jon for a while and then when I come back perhaps I'll live with you and you can look after me.' When I said—for the hundredth time—that I wanted to marry her she said that she didn't even know if she could live with me let alone marry me, and that I would have to wait until she had seen Jon. I said, 'What's Jon got to do with it? How can he help you?' And she turned to me and said: 'You wouldn't understand even if I tried to explain.'

"She came back from Cornwall a month later and said she would marry me. She was transformed. She looked so much better that I hardly recognized her.

"We had a very quiet wedding. Jon and Sophia didn't come and although I thought at the time that it was strange, the full significance never fully occurred to me.

For a while we were very happy—I suppose I had six months of complete happiness, and even now when I look back I would rather have had those six months than none at all. And then Jon came up to town one day from Penzance, and nothing was ever the same again.

"It was a gradual process, the disintegration of our marriage. For the first time I didn't even realize what was happening and then I realized that she was becoming cold, withdrawn. Ironically enough, the colder she became the more I seemed to need her and want her, and the more I wanted her the less she wanted me. In the end she said she wanted a separate bedroom. We quarreled. I asked her if there was some other man, but she just laughed, and when she laughed I shouted out, 'Then why do you see so much of Jon? Why is he always coming up to London? Why do we always get so many invitations to Clougy? Why is it you have to see so much of him?'

"And she turned to me and said, 'Because he's the only man I've ever met who doesn't want to go to bed with me.'

"It was my turn to laugh then. I said, 'He'd want to all right if he wasn't so wrapped up in his wife!'

"And she said, 'You don't understand. There's no question of our going to bed together.'

"It was so strange, the way she said that. I remember feeling that curious sickness one gets in the pit of the stomach the second after experiencing a shock. I said sharply, 'What the hell are you talking about?' And she just said, 'I can't describe how peaceful it is. It's the most perfect thing in all the world.'

"I suppose I knew then that I was frightened. The terrible thing was that I didn't know what I was frightened of. 'You're living with your head in the clouds,' I remember saying to her brutally, trying to shatter my own fear and destroy the barrier between us which she had created. 'You're talking nonsense.' And she said untroubled, as if it were supremely unimportant, 'Think that if you like. I don't care. But no matter what you think, it doesn't alter the fact that sex for me has long since lost all its meaning. It just seems rather ridiculous and unnecessary.' And as if in afterthought she added vaguely, 'I'm so sorry, Michael.' It was funny the way she said that. It had a peculiar air of bathos, and yet it wasn't really bathos at all. 'I'm so sorry, Michael . . .'

"I still couldn't stop loving her. I tried to leave, but I had to go back. I can't even begin to describe what a hell it was. And then we had that final invitation to Clougy, and I resolved that I must talk to Jon and lay my cards on the table. I knew he was absorbed with his wife, and I thought at the time that his relationship with Marijohn would be a much more casual, unimportant thing than her attitude towards him.

"We hadn't been five minutes at Clougy before I realized that Sophia was driving him to the limits of his patience and testing his love beyond all the bounds of endurance. And suddenly, that weekend, his patience snapped and he turned away from her—he'd had enough and could stand no more of her petulance and infidelity. And when he turned away, it was as if he turned to Marijohn.

"It was the most dangerous thing that could have happened; I was beside myself with anxiety, and tried to get Marijohn away, but she refused to go. I tried to talk to Jon but he pretended he hadn't the faintest idea what I was talking about and that there was nothing wrong between him and Marijohn. And then—then of all moments—Sophia had to stumble across what was happening and drag us all towards disaster.

"She'd been having an affair with Max and they'd driven into St. Ives for the afternoon. Jon was in the music room with Marijohn, and rather than make an unwelcome third I went out fishing and tried to think what the hell I was going to do. I didn't come to any conclusion at all. The child came, I remember, and sat talking to me and in some ways I was grateful to him because he took my mind off my troubles. When he went I stayed for a little longer by the shore and then eventually I went back to the house for dinner.

"Sophia and Max were back, and Sophia was looking very uneasy. She talked too much at the start of the meal, and then, when Jon and Marijohn were silent she made no further efforts at conversation. When Jon and Marijohn began to talk to each other at last, ignoring the rest of us entirely, I saw then without a doubt that Sophia had realized what was happening and was going to make trouble.

"The child seemed to sense the tension in the atmosphere for he became very troublesome, and suddenly I felt I had to get out of the room and escape. I took the child upstairs. It was the only excuse I could think of which enabled me to get away, and I stayed upstairs with him for about half an hour, putting him to bed and reading to him. I can't even remember what we read. All I could think of was that Sophia believed Jon intended to be unfaithful to her, and was going to make trouble. My mind was going round and round in circles. Would she divorce Jon? What would she say? How much would come out? How much would it affect Marijohn? Would it succeed in driving Jon and Marijohn more firmly together than ever? What was going to happen? And I went on reading to the child and pretending to him that everything was normal, and inside my heart felt as if it were bursting. . . .

"When I went back downstairs, they were alone in

the music room and there was a record playing on the gramophone. Sophia was in the kitchen with Max. I closed the door and said to Jon, 'Sophia knows—you realize that?' And he said, looking me straight in the eyes, 'Knows what?'

"I said there was no sense in pretending any longer and that the time had come to be perfectly frank with each other. Marijohn tried to interrupt, telling me not to make such an exhibition of myself, but I shut my mind to her and refused to listen. 'You may not be technically committing adultery with my wife,' I said to Jon, 'but you're behaving exactly as if you are, and Sophia isn't going to accept all these airy fairy tales about a relationship with no sex in it. She's going to believe the worst and act accordingly, and in many ways she'd be justified. Whatever your relationship with my wife is, it's a dangerous one that should be stopped—and it must be stopped.'

"They looked at each other. They looked at me. And as they were silent, thinking, I knew instinctively what it was that was so wrong. They were sharing each other's minds. Sophia, close as she might have been to Jon as the result of physical intimacy, was as a stranger to him in the face of that uncanny intangible understanding he shared with Marijohn. Sophia was being forced into the position of outsider—but not by any means which she could recognize or label. For because their relationship was so far beyond her grasp—or indeed the grasp of any ordinary person—it was impossible for her to identify the wrongness in the relationship although it was possible to sense that wrongness did exist.

"Jon said, 'Look Michael—' but he got no further. The door opened and Sophia walked into the room."

He stopped. The sea went on murmuring at the base

of the cliffs, and there was no light as far as the eye could see. The darkness made Sarah more conscious of her dizziness and of her hot, aching eyes.

"Don't tell me any more," she whispered. "Don't. Please."

But he wasn't listening to her.

"What is it?"

"I thought I heard something." He went on listening but presently he relaxed a little. "There was a terrible scene," he said at last. "I can't begin to tell you what was said. It ended with Jon leaving the room and walking out across the lawn. Marijohn went up to her room, and I was left alone with Sophia. I tried to reason with her but she wouldn't listen and in the end she went upstairs to change her shoes before going out. There was some rendezvous with Max on the Flat Rocks, although I didn't know that at the time. I stayed in the drawing-room until I heard her go, and then I went up to my room to find Marijohn but she was no longer there. I stayed there thinking for a long while.

"After Sophia's death, I thought for a time that everything was going to work out at last, but I was too optimistic. Marijohn and Jon had a very long talk together. I don't know what was said, but the upshot of it was that they had decided to part for good. I think Sophia's death—or rather, the scene that preceded her death—had shaken them and they realized they couldn't go on as they were. Jon went to Canada, to the other side of the world, and Marijohn returned with me to London, but she didn't stay long and we never lived together as man and wife again. She went to Paris for a while, came back but couldn't settle down in any place with anyone. I wanted to help her as I knew she was desperately unhappy, but there was nothing I could do and the love I offered her was useless. In the end she turned to religion. She was living in a convent when Jon returned to England a few weeks ago."

He threw away his cigarette. The tip glowed briefly and then died in the darkness.

"So you see," he said slowly at last, "it's quite imperative that you get Jon away from here. It's all happening again, can't you realize that? It's all happening again—we're all here at Clougy, all of us except that woman of Max's, and you've been assigned Sophia's role."

Stone grated on stone; there was the click of a powerful torch, a beam of blinding light.

"Just what the hell are you trying to suggest to my wife, Michael Rivers?" said Jon's hard, dangerous voice from the darkness beyond the torch's beam.

II

"Stay and have dinner with me," said Eve to Justin. "I don't know a soul in this town. Take me somewhere interesting where we can have a meal."

"No," he said, "I have to get back to Clougy." And then, realizing his words might have sounded rude and abrupt, he added hastily, "I promised to get back for dinner."

"Call them and tell them you've changed your mind."

"No, I—" He stopped, blushed, shook his head. His fingers fidgeted with the door handle. "I'm sorry, but I have to get back—it's rather important. There's something I have to talk about with my father."

"About your mother's death?" she said sharply. "Was it something I said? You're sure now that he didn't kill her, aren't you?"

"Yes," he said, and added in a rush: "And I think I know who did." He opened the door and paused to look at her.

She smiled. "Come back when you can," was all she said. "Tell me what happens."

He thanked her awkwardly, his shyness returning for a moment, and then left the room to go downstairs to the hall.

Outside, the golden light of evening was soothing to his eyes. He moved quickly back towards Fish Street, and then broke into a run as he reached the harbor walls and ran down the steps towards the car park. The sea on his right was a dark blue mirror reflecting golden lights from the sky and far away the waves broke in white wavering lines of foam on the sand-dunes of Hayle.

He was panting when he reached the car and had to search for his keys. For one sickening moment he thought he had lost his key-ring, but then he discovered the keys in the inside pocket of his jacket and quickly unlocked the car door. He suddenly realized he was sweating and fear was a sharp prickling tension crawling at the base of his spine.

St. Ives was jammed with the summer tourist traffic leaving the town at the end of the day. It took him quarter of an hour to travel from the car park through the town and emerge on the Land's End road.

He had just reached the lonely stretch of the wild coast road between Morvah and Zennor when the engine spluttered, coughed and was still. He stared at the petrol gauge with incredulous eyes for one long moment, and then, wrenching open the car door he started to run down the road back to Zennor with his heart hammering and pounding in his lungs.

III

Rivers stood up. He didn't hurry. "Put out that torch, for God's sake," he said calmly with a slight air of irritability. "I can't see a thing."

The torch clicked. There was darkness.

"Sarah," said Jon.

She didn't move. She tried to, but her limbs made no response.

"Sarah, what's he been saying to you?"

Rivers took a slight step nearer her and she sensed he had moved to reassure her. Her mouth was dry as if she had run a long way with no rest.

"Sarah!" shouted Jon. "Sarah!"

"For God's sake, Jon," said Rivers, still with his calm air of slight irritability. "Pull yourself together. I suggest we all go back to the house instead of conducting arguments and recriminations on the top of a cliff on a particularly dark Cornish night."

"Go—yourself," said Jon between his teeth and tried to push past him, but Rivers stood his ground.

"Let me by."

"Relax," said Rivers, still calm. "Sarah's perfectly all right but she's had a shock."

"Get out of my—"

They were struggling, wrestling with one another, but even as Sarah managed to stand up Michael made no further attempts to hold Jon back, and stepped aside.

"Sarah," said Jon, trying to take her in his arms. "Sarah—"

She twisted away from him. "Let me go."

"It's not true about Marijohn! Whatever he said to you isn't true!"

She didn't answer. He whirled on Rivers. "What did you tell her?"

Rivers laughed.

"What did you tell her?" He had left Sarah and was gripping Rivers' shoulders. "What did you say?"

"I told her enough to persuade her to leave Clougy as soon as possible. Nothing more."

"What the hell do you—"

"I didn't tell her, for instance, that Sophia's death wasn't accidental. Nor did I tell her that she was pushed down the cliff-path to her death by someone who had a very good motive for silencing her—"

"Why, you—" Jon was blind with rage and hatred. Rivers was forced to fight back in self-defense.

"For Christ's sake, Jon!"

"Jon!" cried Sarah suddenly in fear.

He stopped at once, looking back at her, his chest heaving with exertion. "Did he tell you?" he said suddenly in a low voice. "Did he tell you?"

She leaned back against the rock, too exhausted to do more than nod her head, not even sure what she was affirming. From far away as if in another world she heard Rivers laugh at Jon's panic, but she was conscious only of a great uneasiness prickling beneath her skin.

Jon whirled on Rivers. "How could you?" he gasped. "You love Marijohn. We all agreed ten years ago that no one should ever know· the truth. You said yourself that it would be best for Marijohn if no one ever knew that she and I were—" He stopped.

"Jon," said Rivers a hard warning edge to his voice. "Jon—"

"Yes," cried Sarah in sudden passion. "That you and she were what?"

"That she and I were brother and sister," said Jon exhausted, and then instantly in horror: "My God, you didn't know . . . ?"

IV

Justin managed to get a lift to a garage and paid the mechanic for taking him back to his car with a can of petrol.

It was after sunset. The dusk was gathering.

"Should do the trick," said the mechanic, withdrawing his head from the bonnet. "Give 'er a try."

The starter whined; the engine flickered briefly and died.

"Funny," said the mechanic with interest. "Must be trouble in the carburetor. Petrol not feeding properly. Did the gauge say you was dead out of petrol?"

"No," said Justin. "According to the gauge there was still a little in the tank. I just thought the gauge must have gone wrong."

"Funny," said the mechanic again with a deeper interest, and put his head cautiously back under the bonnet. "Well, now, let me see . . ."

V

Sarah was running. The heather was scratching her legs and the darkness was all around her, smothering her lungs as she fought for breath. And then at last she saw the lighted windows of Clougy and knew she would be able at last to escape from the suffocation of the darkness and the isolation of the Cornish hillsides.

Max Alexander came out into the hall as she stumbled

through the front door and paused gasping by the stairs, her shoulders leaning against the wall, her eyes closed as the blood swam through her brain.

"Sarah! What's happened? What is it?"

She sank down on the stairs, not caring that he should see her tears, and as the scene tilted crazily before her eyes she felt the sobs rise in her throat and shudder through her body.

"Sarah . . ." He was beside her, his arm round her shoulders almost before he had time to think. "Tell me what it is. . . . If there's anything I can do—"

"Where's Marijohn?"

"In the kitchen, I think, clearing up the aftermath of the meal. Why? Do you—"

"Max, can you—would you—"

"Yes?" he said. "What is it? Tell me what you want me to do."

"I—I want to go away. Could you drive me into St. Ives, or Penzance, anywhere—"

"Now?"

"Yes," she whispered, struggling with her tears. "Now."

"But—"

"I want to be alone to think," she said. "I must be able to think."

"Yes, I see. Yes, of course. All right, I'll go and start the car. You'd better pack a suitcase or something, hadn't you?"

She nodded, still blind with tears, and he helped her to her feet.

"Can you manage?"

"Yes," she said. "Yes, thank you."

He waited until she had reached the landing and then he walked out of the open front door and she heard the crunch of his footsteps on the gravel of the drive.

She went to her room. Her smallest suitcase was on

the floor of the cupboard. She was just opening it and trying to think what she should pack when she sensed instinctively that she was no longer alone in the room.

"Max," she said as she swung round, "Max, I—"

It wasn't Max. It was Marijohn.

The silence which followed seemed to go on and on and on.

"What is it?" said Sarah unsteadily at last. "What do you want?"

The door clicked shut. The woman turned the key in the lock and then leaned back against the panels. Somewhere far away the phone started to ring but no one answered it.

"I heard your conversation with Max just now," she said after a while. "I knew then that I had to talk to you."

There was silence again, a deep absolute silence, and then Marijohn said suddenly, "If you leave Jon now it would be the worst thing you could possibly do. He loves you, and needs you. Nothing which happened in the past can ever change that."

She moved then, walking over to the window and staring out at the dark night towards the sea. She was very still.

"That was Sophia's mistake," she said. "He loved and needed her too but she flung it back in his face. It was an easy mistake for her to make, because she never really loved him or understood him. But you do, don't you. I know you do. You're quite different from Sophia. As soon as I saw you, I knew you were quite different from her."

It was difficult to breathe. Sarah found her lungs were aching with tension and her fingernails were hurting the palms of her hands.

"I want Jon to be happy," Marijohn said. "That's all I want. I thought it would make him happy to come down here with you to stay. I thought that if we were to meet again here of all places nothing would happen between us because the memories would be there all the time, warning us and acting as a barrier. But I was wrong and so was he, and there can never be another occasion like this now. He's leaving tomorrow—did you know that? And when he leaves I know I shall never see him again."

She took the curtain in her hands, fingering its softness delicately, her eyes still watching the darkness beyond the pane.

"I don't know what I shall do," she said. "I haven't allowed myself to think much about it yet. You see . . . how can I best explain? Perhaps it's best to put it in very simple language and not try to wrap it up in careful, meaningless phrases. The truth of the matter is that I can't live without Jon, but he can live perfectly well without me. I've always known that. It's got nothing to do with love at all. It's just something that *is*, that exists. I do love Jon, and he loves me, but that's quite irrelevant. We would have this thing which exists between us even if we hated one another. I can best describe it by calling it color. When he's not there, the world is black and gray and I'm only half-alive and dreadfully alone. And when he is there the world is multicolored and I can live and the concept of loneliness is nothing more than a remote unreal nightmare. That's how it affects me, but Jon I know isn't affected in the same way. When I'm not there, he doesn't live in a twilight black-and-white world as I do. He lives in a different world but the world is merely colored differently and although he may miss me he's still able to live a full, normal life. That's why he's been able to marry and find happiness, whereas I know I can never marry again. I should never even have married Mi-

193

chael. But Jon told me to marry. I was unhappy and he thought it was the answer to all my difficulties. I was always unhappy. . . .

"I can't remember when I first discovered this thing. I suppose it was after Jon's parents were divorced and I was taken away from Jon to live in a convent. I knew then how strange the world seemed without him. . . . Then when I was fourteen his father took me away from the convent and I was able to live at his house in London and Jon came back into my life. We both discovered the thing together then. It was rather exciting, like discovering a new dimension. . . . But then his father misunderstood the situation and, thinking the worst, decided to separate us again for a while. That was when I began to have affairs with as many men as I could—anything to bring color back to my gray, black-and-white world. . . . Jon married Sophia. I was glad he was happy, although it was terrible to lose him. I wouldn't have minded so much if I'd liked her, but she was such a stupid little bitch—I couldn't think what he saw in her. . . . I went on, having affair after affair until one day things went wrong and I had a great revulsion—a hatred of men, of life, and of the whole world. It was Jon who cured me. I went down to Clougy to see him and he brought me back to life and promised he'd keep in touch. I married Michael after that. Poor Michael. He's been very good to me always, and I've never been able to give him anything in return."

She stopped. It was still in the room. There was no sound at all.

"Even Michael never understood properly," she said at last. "Even he tended to think I had some kind of illicit relationship with Jon, but it wasn't true. Jon and I have never even exchanged an embrace which could remotely be described as adulterous. The thing we share is quite apart from all that, and I can't see why it should be considered wrong. But Michael thought it was. And Sophia . . . Sophia simply had no understanding of the situation at all. My God, she was a stupid little fool! If ever a woman drove her husband away from her, that woman was Sophia."

A door banged somewhere in the distance. There were footsteps on the stairs, a voice calling Sarah's name.

Marijohn unlocked the door just as Jon turned the handle and burst into the room. "Sarah—" he began and then stopped short as he found himself face to face with Marijohn.

"I was trying to explain to her," she said quietly. "I was trying to tell her about us."

"She already knows. You're too late."

Marijohn went white. "But how—"

"I told her myself," said Jon, and as he spoke Sarah saw them both turn towards her. "I thought Michael had already told her. I'm sure she must have guessed by now that we both had a first-class motive for murdering Sophia."

VI

It was dark on the road but fortunately the mechanic had a torch and could see what he was doing. Justin, glancing around in an agony of impatience, caught sight of a lighted window of a farm-house a few hundred yards from the road and began to move over towards it.

"I won't be long," he called to the mechanic. "I have to make a phone call."

The track was rough beneath his feet and the farmyard when he reached it smelled of manure. The woman who answered the door looked faintly offended when he asked her politely if he could use her telephone, but showed him into the hall and left him alone to make the call.

He dialed the St. Just exchange with an unsteady hand. It seemed an eternity before the operator answered.

"St. Just 584, please."

Another endless space of time elapsed, and then he could hear the bell ringing and his fingers gripped the receiver even tighter then before.

It rang and rang and rang.

"Sorry, sir," said the operator at last, cutting in across the ringing bell, "but there seems to be no reply. . . ."

VII

They were still looking at her, their eyes withdrawn and tense, and it seemed to her as she watched them that their mental affinity was never more clearly visible and less intangible than at that moment when they shared identical expressions.

"What did Sophia threaten to do?" she heard herself say at last, and her voice was astonishingly cool and self-possessed in her ears.

"Surely you can guess," said Jon. "She was going to drag Marijohn's name right across her divorce petition. Can't you picture the revenge she planned in her jealousy, the damage she wanted to cause us both? Can't you imagine the longing she had to hurt and smear and destroy?"

"I see." And she did see. She was beginning to feel sick and dizzy again.

"Marijohn is illegitimate," he said, as if in attempt to

196

explain the situation flatly. "We have the same father. Her mother died soon after she was born and my father —in spite of my mother's protests and disgust—brought her to live with us. After the divorce, he naturally took her away—he had to. My mother only had her there on sufferance anyway."

The silence fell again, deepening as the seconds passed.

"Jon," said Sarah at last. "Jon, did you—"

He knew what she wanted to ask, and she sensed that he had wanted her to ask the question which was foremost on her mind.

"No," he said. "I didn't kill Sophia. You must believe that, because I swear it's the truth. And if you ask why I lied to you, why I always told you Sophia's death was an accident, I'll tell you. I thought Marijohn had killed her. Everything I did which may have seemed like an admission of guilt on my part was in order to protect Marijohn—but although I didn't know it at the time, Marijohn thought *I'd* killed her. In spite of all our mutual understanding, we've both been suffering under a delusion about each other for ten years. Ironic, isn't it?"

She stared at him, not answering. After a moment he moved towards her, leaving Marijohn by the door.

"The scene with Sophia came after supper on the night she died," he said. "Michael was there too. After it was over, I went out into the garden to escape and sat on the swing-seat in the darkness for a long while trying to think what I should do. Finally I went back into the house to discuss the situation with Marijohn but she wasn't there. I went upstairs, but she wasn't there either and when I came downstairs again I met Eve in the hall. She told me Sophia had gone out to the Flat Rocks to meet Max, and suddenly I wondered if Marijohn had gone after Sophia to try and reason with her. I dashed out of the house and tore up the cliff path. I heard Sophia shout 'Let me go!' and then she screamed when I was about a hundred yards from the steps leading down to the Flat Rocks, and on running forward I found Marijohn at the cliff's edge staring down the steps. She was panting as if she'd been running—or struggling. She said that she'd been for a walk along the cliffs towards Sennen and was on her way back home when she'd heard the scream. We went down the steps and found Max bending over Sophia's body. He'd been waiting for her on the Flat Rocks below." He paused. "Or so he said."

There was a pause. Sarah turned to Marijohn. "What a coincidence," she said, "that you should be so near the steps at the time. What made you turn back at that particular moment during your walk along the cliffs and arrive at the steps just after Sophia was killed?"

"Sarah—" Jon was white with anger, but Marijohn interrupted him.

"I could feel Jon wanted me," she said simply. "I knew he was looking for me so I turned back."

Sarah scarcely recognized her voice when she next spoke. It was the voice of a stranger, brittle, hard and cold. "How very interesting," she said. "I've never really believed in telepathy."

"What are you suggesting?" said Jon harshly. "That I'm lying? That Marijohn's lying? That we're both lying?"

Sarah moved past him, opening the door clumsily in her desire to escape from their presence.

"One of you must be lying," she said. "That's obvious. Sophia before she fell called out 'Let me go' which means she was struggling with someone who pushed her to her death. Somebody killed her, and either of you—as you tell me yourself—had an ideal motive."

"Sarah—"

"Let her go, Jon. Let her be."

Sarah was in the corridor now, taking great gulps of air as if she had been imprisoned for a long time in a stifling cell. She went downstairs and out into the drive. The night air was deliciously cool, and as she wandered further from the house the freedom was all around her, a vast relief after the confined tension in that upstairs room.

He was waiting for her by the gate. She was so absorbed in her own emotions and her desire to escape that she never even noticed, as she took the cliff path, that she was being followed.

VIII

"It's a funny thing," said the mechanic when Justin reached the car again, "But I can't make her go. T'aint the carburetor. Can't understand it."

Justin thought quickly. He could get a lift to St. Just and a lift out to the airport, but he would have to walk the mile and a half from the airport down into the valley to Clougy. But anything was better than waiting fruitlessly by the roadside at Zennor. He could try another phone call from the square at St. Just.

"All right," he said to the mechanic. "I'll have to try and get a lift home. Can you fix up for someone from your garage to tow away my car tomorrow and find out what's wrong?"

"Do it right now, if you like. It only means—"

"No, I can't wait now. I'll have to go on ahead." He found a suitable tip and gave it to the man who looked a little astonished by this impatience. "Thank you very much for all your trouble. Goodnight."

"Goodnight to you," said the mechanic agreeably enough, pocketing the tip, and climbed into his shooting brake to drive back along the road towards St. Ives.

IX

Sarah first saw the dark figure behind her when she was half a mile from the house. The cliff path had turned round the hillside so that the lighted windows were hidden from her, and she was just pausing in the darkness to listen to the sea far below and regain her breath after the uphill climb when she glanced over her shoulder and saw the man.

Every bone in her body suddenly locked itself into a tight white fear.

You've been assigned Sophia's role. . . .

The terror was suffocating, wave after wave of hot dizziness that went on and on even after she began to stumble forward along the cliff path. She never paused to ask herself why anyone should want her dead. She only knew in that blind, sickening flash that she was in danger and she had to escape.

But there was no cover on the stark hillside, nowhere to shelter.

It was then that she thought of the rocks below. In the jumbled confusion of boulders at the foot of the cliffs there were a thousand hiding places, and perhaps also another route by the sea's edge back to the cove and the house. If she could somehow find the way down the cliff to the Flat Rocks. . . .

The path forked slightly and remembering her exploring earlier that day, she took the downward path and found the steps cut in the cliff which led to the rocks below.

Her limbs were suddenly awkward; the sea was a roar that receded and pounded in her ears, drowning even the noise of her gasps for breath.

She looked back.

The man was running.

In a panic, not even trying to find the alternative route down the cliff, she scrambled down the steps, clinging to the jutting rocks in the sandy face and sliding the last few feet to the rock below. She started to run forward, slipped, fell. The breath was knocked out of her body and as she pulled herself to her feet she looked up and saw him at the head of the steps above her.

She flattened herself against the large rock nearby, not moving, not breathing, praying he hadn't seen her.

"Sarah?" he called.

He sounded anxious, concerned.

She didn't answer.

He cautiously began to descend the steps.

Let him fall, said the single voice in her mind drowning even the noise of the sea. Let him slip and fall. She couldn't move. If she moved he would see her and she would have less chance of escape.

He didn't like the steps at all. She heard him curse under his breath, and a shower of sand and pebbles scattered from the cliff face as he fumbled his way down uncertainly.

He reached the rock below at last and stood still six feet away from her. She could hear his quick breathing as he straightened his frame and stared around, his eyes straining to pierce the darkness.

"Sarah?" he called again, and added as an afterthought: "It's all right, it's only me."

She was pressing back so hard against the rock that

her shoulder-blades hurt. Her whole body ached with the strain of complete immobility.

He took a step forward and another and stood listening again.

Close at hand the surf broke on the reefs and ledges of the Flat Rocks and was sucked back into the sea again with the undertow.

He saw her.

He didn't move at all at first, and then he came towards her and she started to scream.

Six

I

JUSTIN WAS running, the breath choking his lungs. He was running past the farm down the track to Clougy, not knowing why he was afraid, knowing only that his mother's murderer was at the house and that no one knew the truth except Justin himself and the killer. He didn't even know why his mother had been killed. The apparent motivelessness of the crime nagged his mind as he ran, but he had no doubts about the murderer's correct identity. According to Eve it would only be one person. . . .

He could hear the stream now, could see the hulk of the disused water-wheel on one side of the track, and suddenly he was at Clougy at last and stumbling through the open front door into the lighted hall.

"Daddy!" he shouted, and the word which had lain silent in the back of his vocabulary for ten years was then the first word which sprang to the tip of his tongue. "Where are you? Marijohn!"

He burst into the drawing-room but they weren't there. They weren't in the music room either.

"Sarah!" he shouted. "Sarah!"

But Sarah didn't answer.

He had a sudden premonition of disaster, a white warning flash across his brain which was gone in less than a second. Tearing up the stairs, he raced down the corridor and flung open the door to his father's bedroom.

They were there. They were sitting on the window seat together, and he was vaguely conscious that his father looked drawn and unhappy while Marijohn's calm, still face was streaked with tears.

"Justin! What in God's name—"

"Where's Sarah?" was all he could say, each syllable coming unevenly as he gasped for breath. "Where is she?"

There were footsteps in the corridor unexpectedly, a shadow in the doorway.

"She's gone for a walk with Michael," said Max Alexander.

II

"It's all right," Michael Rivers' voice was saying soothingly from far away. "It's all right, Sarah. It's only me. . . . Look, let's find a better place to sit down. It's too dark here."

She was still shuddering, her head swimming with the shock, but she let him lead her further down towards the sea until they were standing on the Flat Rocks by the water's edge.

"Why did you follow me?" she managed to say as they sat down on a long low rock.

"I saw you leave and couldn't think where on Earth you were going or what you wanted to do. I believe I thought you might even be thinking of committing suicide."

"Suicide?" She stared at him. "Why?" And in the midst of her confusion she was conscious of thinking that in spite of all that had happened, the thought of suicide to escape from her unhappiness and shock had never crossed her mind.

"You've been married—how long? Two weeks? Three? And you discover suddenly that your husband has a rather 'unique' relationship with another woman—"

"We're leaving tomorrow," she interrupted. "Marijohn told me. Jon's decided to leave and never see her again."

"He decided that ten years ago. I'm afraid I wouldn't rely too much on statements like that, if I were you. And what do you suppose your marriage is going to be like after this? He'll never fully belong to you now, do you realize that? Part of him will always be with Marijohn. Good God, I of all people should know what I'm talking about! I tried to live with Marijohn after Jon had first disrupted our marriage, but it was utterly impossible. Everything was over and done with, and there was no going back."

"Stop it!" said Sarah with sudden violence. "Stop it!"

"So in the light of the fact that you know your three-week old marriage is finished, I don't see why you shouldn't think of committing suicide. You're young and unbalanced by grief and shock. You come out here to the Flat Rocks to the sea, and the tide is going out and the currents are particularly dangerous—"

She tried to move but he wouldn't let her go.

"I thought of suicide that weekend at Clougy," he said. "Did you guess that? I went fishing that afternoon by the sea and thought and thought about what I could do. I was out of my mind. . . . And then the child came and talked to me and afterwards I went back to the house. Marijohn was in our bedroom. I knew then how much I loved her, and I knew that I could never share her with any man, even if the relationship she had with him was irreproachable and completely above suspicion. I foresaw that I would be forced to have a scene with Jon in an attempt to tell him that I could stand it no longer and that I was taking Marijohn away. . . . So after dinner we had the final scene. And I was winning. . . . It was going to be all right. Jon was shaken—I can see his expression now. . . . And then, oh Christ, Sophia had to come in, threatening divorce proceedings, threatening exposure to any-- one who would listen—God, she would have destroyed everything! And Marijohn's name smeared all across the Sunday papers and all my friends and colleagues in town saying, 'Poor old Michael—ghastly business. Who would have thought . . .' and so on and so on. . . . All the gossip and publicity, the destruction of Marijohn, of everything I wanted. . . . Sophia was going to destroy my entire world."

"So you killed her."

He looked at her then, his face oddly distant. "Yes," he said. "I killed her. And Jon went away, saying he would never have any further communication with Marijohn, and I thought that at last I was going to have

206

Marijohn back again and that at last I was going to be happy."

His expression changed. He grimaced for a moment, his expression contorted, and when he next spoke she heard the grief in his voice.

"But she wouldn't come back to me," he said. "I went through all that and committed murder to safeguard her and preserve her from destruction, and all she could do was say how sorry she was but she could never live with me again."

The surf broke over the rocks at their feet; white foam flew for a moment in the darkness and disintegrated.

"Sophia knew they were brother and sister," he said. "Not that it mattered. She would have made trouble anyway. But if she had never known they were brother and sister, the scope of her threats would have been narrower and less frightening in its implications. . . But she knew. Very few people did. The relationship had always been kept secret from the beginning in order to spare John's mother embarrassment. Old Towers made out that Marijohn was the child of a deceased younger brother of his. And when they were older they kept it secret to avoid underlining Marijohn's illegitimacy. I always did think it would have been best if Sophia had never known the secret, but Jon told her soon after they were married, so she knew about it from the beginning."

There was another pause. Sarah tried to imagine what would happen if she attempted to break away. Could she reach the cover of the nearby rocks in time? Probably not. Perhaps if she doubled back . . . She turned her head slightly to look behind her, and as she moved, Rivers said,

"And now there's you. You'll divorce Jon eventually. Even if your marriage survives this crisis there'll be others, and then it'll all come out, the relationship with Marijohn, your very natural jealousy—everything. Marijohn's name will be dragged across the petition because like Sophia, you know the truth, and when the time comes for you to want a divorce you'll be embittered enough to use any weapon at your disposal in an attempt to hit back at both of them. And that'll mean danger to Marijohn. Whatever happens I want to avoid that, because of course I still love her and sometimes I can still hope that one day she'll come back. . . . Perhaps she will. I don't know. But whether she comes back or not I still love her just the same. I know that better than anything else in the world."

There was no hope of escape by running behind them across the rock. The way was too jagged and Sarah guessed it would be too easy in the dark to stumble into one of the pools and lagoons beyond the reefs.

"It would be so convenient if you committed suicide," he said. "Perhaps I could even shift the blame on to Jon if murder were suspected. I tried to last time. I planned the death to look like an accident, but I wore a red sweater of Jon's just in case anyone happened to see me go up the cliff path and murder was suspected afterwards. I knew Sophia was meeting Max on the Flat Rocks. I heard Sophia remind him of their rendezvous after supper, and saw Max leave the house later. Then after the scene in the drawing-room when we all went our separate ways, I didn't go up to my bedroom as I told you earlier this evening. Jon went into the garden, Marijohn went to the drawing-room, Sophia went upstairs to change her high-heeled shoes for a pair of canvas beach shoes, and I took Jon's sweater off the chest in the hall and went out ahead of her to the cliffs. I didn't have to wait long before she came out from the house to follow me. . . .

"But they never suspected murder, the slow Cornish police. They talked of accident and suicide, but murder was never mentioned. Nobody knew, you see, of any possible motives. They were all hidden, secret, protected from the outside world. . . ."

"Michael."

He turned to look at her and she was close enough to him to see in the darkness that his eyes were clouded as if he were seeing only scenes of long ago.

"If I said that I wasn't going to divorce Jon and that the secret was safe with me—"

"You'd be wasting your breath, I'm afraid, my dear. I've confessed to you now that I'm a murderer and that's one secret I could never trust you to keep."

She swung round suddenly to face the cliffs. "What's that?"

He swung round too, swiveling his body instinctively, and even as he moved she was on her feet and running away from him in among the rocks to escape.

He shouted something and then was after her and the rocks were the towering tombstones of a nightmare and the roar of the sea merged with the roaring of the blood in her ears. The granite grazed her hands, tore at her stockings, bruised her feet through the soles of her shoes. She twisted and turned, scrambling amongst the rocks, terrified of coming up against a blank wall of rock or falling into a deep gulley. And still he came after her, gaining slowly every minute, and her mind was a blank void of terror depriving her of speech and voice.

When she was at the base of the cliff again she caught her foot in a crevice and the jolt wrenched her ankle and tore off her shoe. She gave a cry of pain, the sound wrenched involuntarily from her body, and as the sound was carried away from her on the still night air she saw the pin-prick of light above her on the cliff-path.

"Jon!" she screamed, thrusting all her energy into that one monosyllable. "Jon! Jon!"

And then Rivers was upon her and she was fighting for her life, scratching, clawing, biting in a frenzy of self-preservation. The scene began to blur before her eyes, the world tilted crazily. She tried to scream again but no sound came, and as the energy ebbed from her body she felt his fingers close on her throat.

There was pain. It was a hot red light suffocating her entire brain. She tried to breathe and could not. Her hands were just slackening their grip on his body when there was a sound far above her, and the pebbles started to rattle down the cliff face, flicking across her face like hail stones.

She heard Rivers gasp something, and then he was gone and she fell back against the rock.

The blackness when it came a second later was a welcome release from the swimming nightmare of terror and fear.

III

When she awoke, there was a man bending over her, and although it seemed that an eternity had passed since Rivers had left her, she learned afterwards that she had been unconscious for less than a minute. The man was frantic. There was sweat on his forehead and fear in his eyes and he kept saying, "Sarah, Sarah, Sarah" as if his mind would not allow him to say anything else.

She put up her hand and touched his lips with her fingers.

"Is she all right?" said another vaguely familiar voice from close at hand. "Where the hell is Rivers?"

The man whose lips she had touched stood up. "Stay here with Sarah, Max. Have you got that? Don't leave her alone for a moment. Stay with her."

"Jon," her voice said. "Jon."

He bent over her again. "I'm going to find him," he said to her gently. "Justin's gone after him already. Max'll look after you."

"He—he killed Sophia, Jon. . . . He told me—"

"I know."

He was gone. One moment he was there and the next moment he had moved out of her sight and she was alone with Alexander. He was breathing very heavily, as if the sudden violent exercise had been too much for him.

"Max—"

"Yes, I'm here." He sat down beside her, still panting with exertion, and as he took her hand comfortingly in his she had the odd instinctive feeling that he cared for her. The feeling was so strange and so illogical that she dismissed it instantly without a second thought, and instead concentrated all her mind on the relief of being alive.

And as they waited together at the base of the cliffs, Jon was sprinting over the Flat Rocks to the water's edge, the beam of the torch in his hand warning him of the gulleys and the crevices, the reefs and lagoons.

By the water's edge he paused.

"Justin!"

There was an answering flicker of a torch further away, a muffled shout.

Jon moved forward again, leaping from rock to rock, slithering past seaweed and splashing in diminuitive rock pools. It took him two minutes to reach his son.

"Where is he?"

"I don't know." Justin's face was white in the torch-light, his eyes dark and huge and ringed with tiredness.

"You lost sight of him?"

"He was here." He gestured with his torch. They were standing on a squat rock, and six feet below them the sea was sucking and gurgling with the motions of the tide. "I saw him reach this rock and then scramble over it until he was lost from sight."

Jon was silent. Presently he shone his torch up and down the channel below, but there was nothing there except the dark water and the white of the surf.

"Could he—do you think he would have tried to swim round to the cove?"

"Don't be a bloody fool."

The boy hung his head a little, as if regretting the stupidity of his suggestion, and waited wordlessly for the other man to make the next move.

"He couldn't have fallen in the darkness," said Jon after a moment. "When you reach the top of a rock you always stop to look to see what's on the other side. And if he had slipped into this channel he could have clambered out on to the other side—unless he struck his head on the rocky floor, and then we'd be able to see his body."

"Then—"

"Perhaps you're right and he went swimming after all. . . . We'd better search these rocks here just to make sure, I suppose. You take that side and I'll take this side."

But although they searched for a long while in the darkness they found no trace of Michael Rivers, and it was many weeks before his body was finally recovered from the sea.

IV

"What'll happen?" said Justin to his father. "What shall we do?"

They were in the drawing-room at Clougy again. It was after midnight, and the tiredness was aching through Justin's body in great throbbing waves of exhaustion. Even when he sat down the room seemed to waver and recede dizzily before his eyes.

"We'll have to call the police."

"You're mad, of course," said Alexander from the sofa. "You must be. What on Earth are you going to say to the police? That Michael's dead? We don't know for sure that he is. That Michael tried to kill Sarah? The first question the police are going to ask is why the hell should Michael, a perfectly respectable solicitor, a pillar of society, suddenly attempt to murder your wife. My dear Jon, you'll end up by getting so involved that the police will probably think we're all in one enormous conspiracy to pull wool over their eyes. They'll ask you why, if you *knew* your first wife had been murdered, you didn't say so at the time. They'll ask you all sorts of questions about Marijohn and your reasons for wanting to protect her. They'll probe incessantly for motives—"

"For Christ's sake, Max!"

"Well, stop talking such God almighty rubbish."

"Are you scared for your own skin or something?"

"Oh God," said Alexander wearily, and turned to the boy hunched in the armchair. "Justin, explain to your father that if he goes to the police now Sophia—and probably Michael too—have both died in vain. Ask him

213

if he really wants Sarah's name smeared all across the Sunday papers. 'Canadian millionaire in murder mystery. Horror on the Honeymoon.' God, can't you imagine the headlines even now? 'Sensation! Millionaire's first wife *murdered!* Millionaire helping the police in their inquiries.' It would be intolerable for you all, Jon—for Sarah, for Justin, for Marijohn—"

The door opened. He stopped as Marijohn came into the room.

"How is she?" said Jon instantly. "Is she asking for me? Is she all right?"

"She's asleep. I gave her two of my sleeping tablets." She turned away from him and moved over towards ·the boy in the corner. "Justin darling, you look quite exhausted. Why don't you go to bed? There's nothing more you can do now."

"I—" He faltered, looking at his father. "I was wondering what's going to happen. If you call the police—"

"Police?" said Marijohn blankly. She swung round to face Jon. "Police?"

"Tell him he's crazy, Marijohn."

"Look, Max—"

There they go again, thought Justin numbly. More arguments, more talk. Police or no police, what to tell and what not to tell, Michael's death or disappearance and what to do about it. And I'm so very very tired. . . .

He closed his eyes for a second. The voices became fainter and then suddenly someone was stooping over him and there was an arm round his shoulders and the cold rim of the glass against his lips. He drank, choked and opened his eyes as the liquid burnt his throat.

"Poor Justin," said the voice he had loved so much ten years ago. "Come on, you're going to bed. Drank the rest of the brandy and we'll go upstairs."

There was fire in his throat again. The great heaviness

in his limbs seemed to lessen fractionally and with his father's help he managed to stand up and moved over to the door.

"I'm all right now," he heard himself say in the hall. "Sorry to be a nuisance."

"I'll come upstairs with you."

There seemed more stairs than usual, an endless climb to the distant plateau of the landing, but at last they were in the bedroom and the bed was soft and yielding as he sank down on it thankfully.

"I'm all right," he repeated automatically, and then his shirt was eased gently from his body and the next moment the cool pajama jacket brushed his skin.

"I'm afraid I've been very selfish," said his father's voice. "I haven't said a word of thanks to you since you arrived back and all I could do down on the Flat Rocks was to be abrupt and short-tempered."

"It—it doesn't matter. I understand."

"I'll never forget that it was you who saved Sarah. I want you to know that. If Sarah had died tonight—"

"She'll be all right, won't she? She's going to be all right?"

"Yes," said Jon. "She's going to be all right."

The sheets were deliciously white, the pillow sensuously soft and yielding. Justin sank back, pulling the coverlet across his chest and allowing his limbs to relax in a haze of comfort and peace.

He never even heard his father leave the room.

When he awoke it was still dark but someone had opened the door of his room and the light from the landing was shining across the foot of his bed.

"Who's that?" he murmured sleepily, and then Marijohn was stooping over him and he twisted round in bed so that he could see her better. "What's happened?"

he said, suddenly very wide awake, his brain miraculously clear and alert. "Have you called the police?"

"No." She sat down on the edge of the bed and for a moment he thought she was going to kiss him but she merely touched his cheek lightly with her fingertips. "I'm sorry I woke you up. I didn't mean to disturb you. Jon's just gone to bed and Max is still downstairs drinking the last of the whisky. We've been talking for nearly three hours."

He sat up a little in bed. "Haven't you decided anything?"

She looked at him and he thought he saw her smile faintly, but the light was behind her and it was difficult for him to see her face.

"You're leaving tomorrow—you and Sarah and Jon," she said and there was a curious dull edge to her voice which he didn't fully understand. "You'll go straight to London and catch the first plane to Canada. Max and I are going to handle the police."

He stared at her blankly. "How?" he said. "What are you going to tell them?"

"Very little. Max is going to drive Michael's car up past the farm and abandon it on the heath near the airport. Then tomorrow or the day after I'm going to phone the police and tell them that I'm worried about Michael and think he may have committed suicide—I'm going to say that Max and I have found Michael's car abandoned on the heath after you all departed for London. Our story is going to be that Michael came down here in the hope of persuading me to go back to him, and when I refused—finally and forever—there was a scene which ended in him leaving the house and driving away. We shall say he threatened suicide before he left. Then the police can search for him as thoroughly as they wish, and when his body is eventually recovered—

as I suppose it must be, even on this rocky coast—it'll lend support to our story."

"Supposing Michael isn't dead?"

"He must be. Jon is convinced of it. Michael had nothing left to live for, nothing at all."

"But . . ." He hesitated, trying to phrase what he wanted to say. Then: "Why is it so vital that the police don't know the truth from start to finish?" he blurted out at last. "I mean, I know the scandal would be terrible, but—"

"There are reasons," she said. "Your father will tell you."

"But why did Michael try to kill Sarah? And why did he kill my mother? I don't—"

"He wanted to protect me," she said, her voice suddenly flat and without life. "It was all for me. Your father will explain everything to you later when you're all far away in Canada."

He still stared at her. "I couldn't see why he was the murderer," he repeated at last. "I knew he must have been the murderer but I couldn't see why."

"What did Eve tell you? What did she say that suddenly made you realize Michael was guilty?"

"I—I persuaded her to talk to me about her own memories of that weekend at Clougy, and her memories, when I pieced them together with my own, spelled the real sequence of events." He paused to collect his thoughts, thinking of Eve and the little room in St. Ives above the blue of the bay. "I thought my father had killed my mother because I followed a man with a red sweater up the cliff-path and saw him push my mother to her death in the darkness. . . . As soon as I'd seen her fall I ran away up the hillside and over the hill-top to Clougy. I didn't take the cliff-path back to the house because I was afraid my father would see me, so I nev-

217

er discovered that the man in the red sweater wasn't my father at all. But I think Michael must have returned to the house by a similar route to the one I took, because neither of you, coming from Sennen, nor my father, coming from Clougy along the cliff-path, saw either Michael or myself. My father told me tonight that you and he had met by the steps soon after my mother fell.

"When I left the house to follow the man in the red sweater I met Eve—she was coming up the path from the beach just as I was about to take the fork which led up on the cliffs. I hid from her, and she didn't see me.

"This afternoon she told me what had happened to her that evening. She said that when she reached the house again after I'd seen her she met my father. That proved to me that the man in the red sweater couldn't have been my father, and she also remembered he wasn't wearing a sweater when she saw him and that the red sweater he'd worn earlier in the evening had been removed from the chest in the hall.

"That meant the man had to be either Michael or Max. And according to Eve, it couldn't possibly have been Max because she'd seen him go off along the cliff-path to the Flat Rocks some while before she passed me on her way back to the house. She said they had quarreled at the spot where the path from Clougy forks, one track leading up on to the cliffs and one leading down to the cove, and afterwards he had gone off up the cliff-path to wait for my mother—Eve saw him go. Then she sat down by the fork in the path to try to pull herself together and decide what she should do. She would have seen Max if he had come back from the cliffs, but he didn't come back. And the man in the red sweater, whom I followed had started out *from the house* a few minutes before I saw Eve coming back up the path to Clougy where she was to meet my father. So the man had to be Michael. My father was still at the house and Max had already gone out to the Flat Rocks. There was no one else it could possibly be."

"I see." She was silent for a moment, and he wondered what she was thinking. And then she was standing up, smoothing the skirt of her dress over her hips automatically, and moving towards the door again. "You'd better get some more sleep," she said at last. "I mustn't keep you awake any longer."

She stepped across the threshold, and as she turned to close the door and the light slanted across her face, something in her expression made him call out after her.

But she did not hear him.

V

Max had just finished the whisky when Marijohn went downstairs to lock up and switch off the lights. A half-smoked cigarette was between his fingers and as she came into the room the ash dropped from the glowing tip to the carpet.

"Hullo," he said, and he didn't sound very drunk. "How's my fellow-conspirator?"

She drew the curtains back, not answering, and reached up to fasten the bolt on the French windows.

"You know why I'm doing it, don't you?" he said sardonically. "I'm not doing it for you or for Jon. Between you you've destroyed a good man and were indirectly responsible for Sophia's death. You deserve all you get. So I'm not doing this for you. I'm doing this for the girl because I don't see why she should suffer any more than she's suffered already. Quixotic, isn't it? Rather amusing. But then I've always been a fool over women. . . . Lord, what a fool I was over Sophia! I wanted her dead just as much as everyone else did, did you ever realize that? I told Sarah this afternoon that I felt sorry for Sophia, and so I did—to begin with. But I left several details out of my story to Sarah; I never told her that Sophia was trying to force me into taking her away to London with me, never mentioned that Sophia was threatening me, never hinted that it was I, not Sophia, who suggested the rendezvous on the Flat Rocks so that I could try and make her see reason. . . . And once she was dead, of course, I said nothing, never breathing a word of my suspicions to anyone, because I had a strong motive for wanting her dead and in any police murder inquiry I would naturally be one of the chief suspects. . . . And even now you won't have to worry in case I decide to change my mind and say too much to the police some time in the future, because I know for a fact that I haven't long to live and when I die you'll all be quite safe, you and Jon, Sarah and the boy. . . . The boy will have to know the full story, of course. I can't say I envy Jon having to explain. . . . You're fond of the boy, aren't you? I suppose it's because he reminds you of Jon."

Yes, said a voice in her brain instantly in a sudden flare of grief, and no doubt I shall always have to share him just as I've had to share Jon. Aloud she said, "I've no mental affinity with Justin at all. He doesn't remind me of Jon as much as all that."

There was a pause before Alexander said, "And what will you do? You won't stay here longer than you can help, will you?"

"No," she said. "Jon wants me to sell Clougy. He says he never wants to see the place again."

"Poor old Jon," said Alexander inconsequentially, swallowing the dregs of his whisky. "Who would have thought the day would have come when he would say he never wanted to see Clougy again? He'll be saying next that he never wants to see you again either."

"He doesn't have to say that," said Marijohn, and the tears were like hot needles behind her eyes. "I already know."

VI

When Sarah awoke it was dim and she could see that there was a white mist swirling outside the window beyond the chink in the curtains. She stirred. Memory returned suddenly in sickening flashes of consciousness, and even as she reached for him instinctively, Jon was pulling her close to him and burying his face in her hair as he kissed her.

"How are you feeling?"

She pressed against him, savoring his nearness and her own security. "Jon . . . Jon . . ."

"We're leaving with Justin after breakfast," he said. "Then as soon as we get to London we're flying home to Canada. I'll explain later how Max and Marijohn are going to cope with the police—you don't have to worry about anything at all."

She put her hand to his face and traced the outline of his jaw as she kissed him on the mouth.

"I love you," he said in between her kisses, and his

voice was unsteady so that it didn't sound like his voice at all. "Do you hear? I love, love, love you, and you're never never going to have to go through anything like this again."

"Will we come back to England?" she murmured. The question didn't seem very important somehow but she had a feeling it should nevertheless be asked.

"No," he said, his voice firm and positive again. "Never."

"Oh." She sighed, half-wondering why she had no feeling of sadness. "We must find time to say good-bye to your mother before we leave," she said as an afterthought. "I feel sorry for her in some ways. I'm sure she'll miss Justin terribly."

"She'll get over it." His mouth was hardening again. "Like most beautiful women she's egocentric enough to care for no one deeply except herself."

"That's nonsense, Jonny, and you know it!" She felt almost cross. "It's obvious to any outsider that she cares very deeply for you—no, I don't care what you say! I know I'm right! We must invite her out to Canada to visit us. She's got plenty of money so she'll be able to come whenever she likes. And anyway I think Justin should have the opportunity to keep in touch with his grandmother—after all, she brought him up, didn't she? In spite of the row they had when you offered him the job in Canada, I'm sure he must be very fond of her. Before we fly back to Canada we must call on her and arrange something."

Jon's mouth was still a hard stubborn line. "Sarah—"

She slipped her hand behind his head and pressed his face to hers to kiss the stubbornness from his expression. "Please, Jon!"

The victory came in less than five seconds. She felt him relax, saw his eyes soften, felt his mouth curve in a smile, and she knew then for the first time that there would be no more dread of the Distant Mood, no more tension and worry because she did not understand or could not cope with his changes of humor. When he bent over her a moment later and she felt the love in every line of his frame flow into hers, she knew he would never again belong to anyone else except her.

Epilogue

WHEN THEY HAD all gone and she was alone in the still quiet house, Marijohn sat down at the desk in the drawing-room and took a clean sheet of notepaper and a pen.

She sat thinking for a long while. It was very peaceful. Outside the sky was blue and the stream rushed past the waterwheel at the end of the drive.

She dipped her pen in the ink.

"My darling Jon," she wrote quickly at last with firm, resolute strokes of the pen. "By the time you read this, you will be come in Canada in the midst of your new life. I know there's so much for you there, more now than ever before, as both Sarah and Justin will be with you and in time Sarah will have children of her own. I want you to know first and foremost how glad I am about this, because almost more than anything else on Earth I want you to be happy and to lead a rich, full, worthwhile life.

"I have decided to go back to the only world I think I could ever live in now, the world of Anselm's Cross —or of any convent anywhere. I did think of avoiding this by traveling abroad, Jon, just as you suggested, but I don't think I would find peace abroad any more than I would find peace here at Clougy.

"When I look back I can see how clearly the fault was mine. In a way, it was I who killed Sophia and I who killed Michael and I who almost killed Sarah. I ruined Michael's life and very nearly yours as well. You could forgive me for both I expect, but I know you'll never really forgive me for what happened to Sarah that night. Max always said *you* were the one who was the constant source of danger to everyone around you, but he was wrong. I was the source of danger, not you. Everything I touch seems to turn into a disaster. If you're honest with yourself you'll see that as clearly as I see it now.

"You did talk when we parted of perhaps seeing me again in the very distant future, but Jon darling, I know you so well and I know when you're lying to save me pain. I shall never see you again, not because you think it's better for us to be apart or because you owe it to Sarah or for any other noble reason, but because you *don't want* to see me—because you know, just as I know, that it was through me that Sarah was nearly killed and your second marriage nearly wrecked as utterly as your first, and you never want to run the risk of that happening again. I don't blame you; in a way, the knowledge that I'll never see you again helps me to see more clearly which course I now have to take.

"I've just three things left to say. Don't pity me, don't blame yourself, and don't ever try to communicate with me, even out of kindness, in the years to come.

"All my love, darling, now and always, and all the happiness you could ever wish for,

"Your own,

"Marijohn"